NUDGING FATE

After being widowed by a car accident Emma Dane decides to make a new life for herself and her young daughter, Jenny, back in the idyllic Norfolk countryside of her childhood. She finds a post teaching at the local school and although she quickly makes friends, the local vet seems determined to be rude and dismissive every time she sees him. Yet, despite his coldness, she can't seem to get him out of her mind . . .

MARJORIE SANTER

◆

NUDGING FATE

Complete and Unabridged

LINFORD
Leicester

First published in Great Britain in 2009

First Linford Edition
published 2009

British Library CIP Data

Santer, Marjorie.
    Nudging fate.- -(Linford romance library)
    1. Widows- -Fiction. 2. Women teachers- -Fiction.
    3. Veterinarians- -Fiction. 4. Norfolk (England)- -
    Fiction. 5. Love stories. 6. Large type books.
    I. Title II. Series
    823.9'2–dc22

    ISBN 978–1–84782–949–8

Published by
F. A. Thorpe (Publishing)
Anstey, Leicestershire

Set by Words & Graphics Ltd.
Anstey, Leicestershire
Printed and bound in Great Britain by
T. J. International Ltd., Padstow, Cornwall

This book is printed on acid-free paper

For my dear friend, Sally

1

There must have been something in the flickering firelight that triggered off a memory. It's strange how the smallest and most inconsequential things can bring past experiences most vividly to life. That firelight brought back another time, another place of thirty years ago. It was just such another bleak winter's evening, the sleet battering at the windows and a blustery wind buffeting the trees in the garden and, like now, I was sitting by the fire . . . Waiting.

Jenny, only three years old then, was fast asleep in bed and I remembered how I went to the window more than once and, shielding my eyes, peered out into the wild and wintry night. I shivered at the memories for they still haunted me a little although I must admit that I had given them little thought for a long, long while.

Somehow they were staying with me this evening and, as I leaned back into the comfort of my armchair, they would not go away. I can remember every detail of that night and probably every twist and turn of the time that followed for it was such a turning point in my life.

★　★　★

I had been sitting close to the fire, trying to get warm, when there was a quiet knock on the door with almost a hesitancy about it. I looked up at the clock on the wall. Two-thirty in the morning and Jimmy must have forgotten his key again. With, by now, a familiar little feeling of dread at the back of my mind, I went to open the door.

Nothing prepared me for the sight of the burly policeman standing there.

'Mrs. Dane?'

'Yes.' My voice came out in a whisper. I caught sight of a woman police officer behind him and it was as if an icy finger traced a pathway down my spine.

2

I reached out a hand. 'What's happened? Has . . . has there been an . . . an accident?'

For this worry had been imprisoned at the back of my mind for some time now, knowing how Jimmy loved the fast lane . . . in more ways than one . . . and also how many times of late he had returned home in the early hours the worse for drink. When I had begged him to be more careful I had only got the rough edge of his tongue and once, dreadfully, a sharp blow across my shoulders which had knocked me to the floor. He had been filled with remorse the next morning, having only a hazy idea of what had happened but knowing it had been bad.

'I think we had better come in, please, Mrs. Dane.'

'Oh, yes, yes . . . of course. But please . . . ' I gazed up at him, feeling stupidly numb.

The policewoman came from behind him and took my arm.

'Sit down Mrs. Dane. I'm so very

sorry but I'm afraid we have some very bad news for you.'

She sat me down on the nearest chair and they told me as gently as they could of the accident. The accident that had not only involved Jimmy but a girl also. A girl who had been in the car with him and, as I was to find out later, had been with him many times before. Never in a million years would I have suspected him. Which just goes to show what a blinkered fool I was. Still adolescent almost.

I grew up very quickly that night.

They had both been drinking and Jimmy had always been a reckless driver. I was told that the car had skidded at a particularly sharp bend and ploughed into a brick wall.

The policewoman who had pulled up a chair to sit opposite me leaned forward and patted my hand.

'They wouldn't have known anything,' she said. 'They were killed instantly.'

That was supposed to comfort me?

They must have thought I was weird because I just stared at them. I couldn't seem to get my head round it or them or anything. Jimmy couldn't be completely gone . . . just like that.

'Is there anyone we can call for you?' she asked but I shook my head. I had lost both my parents when I was only five years old. A plane crash then, while they were on holiday abroad. My dear Aunt Maggie who had brought me up was long gone. Jimmy's parents lived in France. They would have to be told of course but were no help to me now. Nor had they ever been for that matter.

But there was Peggy, my good and best friend and she arrived like a small whirlwind to fling her arms round me and hold me close. And then I did let go.

After those dreadful first weeks following Jimmy's death I somehow pulled myself together. I grieved for him. Of course I grieved for him but perhaps I sorrowed more for the loss of the young husband I had trusted and been happy with and for the inescapable fact that now there would never be any chance of making our marriage work. But, as everyone pointed out, trying to be helpful I suppose, life goes on and I had my darling Jenny to consider and for her sake I had to pin a smile on my face whenever possible.

What I would have done without Peggy, I shudder to think. She was an absolute lifeline. We had known each other since our first days of teaching as we both started at Norton Primary School in a Manchester suburb at the same time and had shared both difficult and good times . . . and most of our secrets. With no hesitation at all she insisted that Jenny and I should move in with her. She lived in a comfortable little semi that her parents had left her, so there was room for us and I was grateful. A few months later I had sold our house and practically all the furniture, only too glad to be away from a place that now only reminded me of shattered hopes and dreams, of sadness tinged irrevocably with bitterness.

'It's only for a little while, Pegs,' I had said. 'Just until I have decided what to do.'

Once the hefty mortgage had been repaid as well as other bills that had cropped up from all over the place, funds were getting a bit low. I had given up my job when Jenny was born and in spite of Jimmy's grumbling had held fast to the promise I had made to myself to be at home for Jenny until she started school. Now it looked as if I would have to go back to work and find somewhere for Jenny to be looked after. Not a happy thought.

I was sitting at the kitchen table one afternoon surrounded by papers when I heard the door open and Peggy call out.

'Hi, troops. If you value your life, get that kettle on. Ooh, what a day!'

She flung a heavy bag of books onto one chair and herself on to another and Jenny came at a run and clambered on to her knee.

'Jenny, love, let your Auntie Pegs get her breath.'

'Oh, that's O.K. Em. A hug is just what I need right now.' She eyed my pile of paperwork. 'What are you doing? Sorting out the National Debt?'

I grinned at her ruefully as I held the kettle under the tap.

'That's what it feels like, Pegs. I shall have to get myself a job . . . and quick. I don't suppose they want any supply teachers at Norton, do they?'

She shook her head. 'You know, Em, I've been thinking about that. I don't see why we can't let things go on as they are doing for a while longer.'

I began to protest but she held up her hand.

'Hang on, let me finish. Now you don't really want to go back to teaching until Jenny is ready for school. Look how you stood up to Jimmy about that and I think you were right. And I have never been so comfortable for a long while with you looking after the house and everything . . . and the cooking.

Honestly, Emma, I just love the meals you do. You can pay your way up to a point if you want to. If it will make you feel better. What do you say?'

She only ever called me 'Emma' when she was serious about something, so I looked across at her and thought hard.

'I feel as if I'm taking advantage.'

'What utter rubbish. There is one drawback though,' and I must have looked anxious for she chuckled. 'I shall get as fat as a little pig on your cooking,' and then, in the same breath, enquired guilessly, 'I suppose you wouldn't have a piece of that delectable coffee cake knocking about, would you?'

I turned to the cupboard behind me and reached for the cake tin and we both burst out laughing.

So the weeks lengthened into months and the months into over a year. I took over all the household chores and paid my way and in return Jenny and I had a roof over our heads and no worries. It had proved to be a happy arrangement. Peggy adored little Jenny and she, in turn, loved her Auntie Pegs. Peggy insisted that she had never been so well fed and comfortable for years and was thoroughly enjoying the relief from household tasks.

Christmas had come and gone once more and I had rolled up my sleeves and just about turned the little house we shared inside out. But nothing seemed to ease the restlessness that simmered away inside me. One night as I lay sleepless, with the bright moonlight pushing its way through the flimsy curtains, I allowed thoughts of the past . . . the unhappy ones . . . to come flooding back into my mind. Now I may be indecisive about a lot of things but I have managed to control those particular thoughts to quite an amazing degree. I pride myself on that. Usually when those 'dragons' . . . for that is how I thought of them . . . began to rear their heads I could deal with them pretty smartish and push them into obscurity at the back of my mind. I found work to do, switched on the radio or the telly or reached for a book. If there was no-one about I sometimes even burst into song! Did anything rather than think. It didn't work at first but eventually the dragons were, if not tamed, then at least subdued. And I survived.

I lay there blaming the moonshine that flooded the room for my sleeplessness and gradually and, oh so subtly, the dragons crept nearer, scaly claw by scaly claw until they had me in their grip and I was back in the past.

I drifted back in time to the birth of my dearest Jenny, then further back to when I knew I was first pregnant and Jimmy had been so bitter because I had insisted on giving up my teaching job which paid for so many extras.

When I told him that I had handed in my notice and not just applied for maternity leave he hadn't believed me at first.

I remembered his words so well.

'You can't be serious,' he had said. 'We can't afford it. You've gone off your rocker.'

Then his scowl cleared and he tilted his head and gazed at me with those melting brown eyes that usually had the effect of putting me in the melting pot as well.

'Women do have some odd reactions when they're pregnant, love. You'd better get another letter off to the Ed. Office quick and put things right before it's too late and someone else steps into your shoes.'

I gritted my teeth and insisted that it wasn't some mental lapse and I didn't want to go back to teaching until the baby was school age.

Then it was as if all hell had broken loose. At least, that is what it felt like.

Over and over again I had tried to persuade him that it would only mean doing without luxuries for a while. I remember pleading with him.

'You've got a good job, darling. We shan't want for anything. It will only mean cutting out the holidays abroad and theatres and parties and things like that and we wouldn't be able to do those sort of things with a young baby in any case. I'll give up my car because if I'm going to be at home I shan't need it and we can manage with yours and we'll make it last us a bit longer.'

That had been entirely the wrong thing to say. Jimmy liked to change his car every year and had planned to invest in a sleek Jag that he had seen a few weeks before.

As if a mask had slipped, I saw a side of his nature that I had never seen before. Admittedly he hadn't been best pleased when I had first told him I was pregnant, blaming me for carelessness with our family planning. I really hadn't been careless but I felt so guilty. Heaven alone knows why. Eventually his ill-humour had passed and I remember thinking naively that it would only be a passing phase. I was so overjoyed at the thought of the baby that I didn't realise that Jimmy in no way shared my joy.

Up till then, our life together had been one of constant partying and entertainment, and if there had been times when I found it difficult and tiring to cope with my teaching job in the way that I wanted to and also to handle Jimmy's fast pace of living in the way that kept him happy, then I kept it to myself and did the best I could.

His high-powered job with a prestigious advertising firm kept us in the fast lane and it was a bit like walking a tightrope.

I had first met him at a colleague's birthday bash. I hadn't really wanted to go. My hair needed washing, I'd laddered my last pair of decent tights and there was a mountain of school work needing attention. It was one of those days. But Peggy pushed me into it so there I was with a g. and t. in one hand and a chicken leg in the other, looking across the room at this tall broad-shouldered man with smooth dark hair and a wicked grin. He was surrounded by a bevy of glamorous females apparently hanging on his every word. Then he turned his head and the grin was aimed straight at me so I smiled back.

The birthday girl came up behind me and murmured in my ear.

'I can see where you're looking, Emma, but watch out. Jimmy Dane. He eats little girls like you for breakfast . . . and then spits them out.'

Her warning was completely useless. He came across and held out his hand and I was lost.

Why me? I often thought, when he could have any gorgeous girl he wanted. I said that to Peggy once and her reply made me shake my head at her.

'Look in the mirror, Em,' she said.

I asked Jimmy and in one of his rare serious moments he said, 'You're good for me, Em. Too good probably.'

'We're good for each other,' I had answered and gave myself up to his kisses again.

I had been besotted with him. Twenty, and, believe it or not, in love for the very first time. I was a pushover.

He loved me too. I know he did at first. But I also know now that I had been a green girl, dazzled by a handsome face and physique and a spurious maturity and sophistication. I simply wasn't aware of this in the beginning and all that mattered to me was Jimmy's approval and admiration.

We were married four months after that fateful party.

My thoughts moved on to that incredible day when, a few months on into my pregnancy, the new life I held within me had moved and fluttered against my hand as I was pulling on my clothes. My world tilted on its axis and I knew in that heart-stirring, exhilarating moment that my life would never be the same again. That was when I made a promise to my unborn baby. No-one else was going to be in charge of his, or her first years. There were going to be no childminders or nurseries. I thanked the fates with all my heart that I was in the fortunate position of being able to make that promise. I knew that I could give up work for a while without causing any financial hardship for Jimmy or myself. Trustingly I had thought that Jimmy would agree with me.

How wrong I had been.

The quality of our life together improved for a while after Jenny was born. Maybe Jimmy felt a bit guilty about the way he had treated me. I don't know. During the latter part of my pregnancy he wouldn't even walk down the street with me, saying I embarrassed him. Well, who would want to go out with a beached whale? I can't really blame him for that. My social life came to a full stop. Not that I minded at all but I did wish that he would stay in with me a bit more. He went out most evenings but then, that was Jimmy and I understood.

Our little girl was such a lovely baby and Jimmy made quite a fuss of her at first. Sadly, the novelty of being a new and supposedly proud father soon wore off. As Jenny began to toddle round he began to put more and more pressure on me to return to teaching.

'You've got a good job, Jimmy,' I had pleaded. 'I don't need to go back to work just yet, surely? Please let's wait until she starts school and then I will, I promise you.'

His angry retorts and punishing silences caused me to see, sadly, that the dashing, sophisticated young man I had married was, at heart, a spoilt and immature boy. But boys grow up I told myself determinedly. He'll find Jenny more interesting when she's a bit older. We'll both love him such a lot and perhaps responsibility will bring out the good in him which I know is there. We'll forget all about this bad patch later on when there is more money coming in. He's just frustrated, that's all. So I had comforted myself when he flung out of the house in a temper time and again, leaving me in an agony of indecision.

I used to walk round the house just hugging Jenny to me, worrying and trying to feel that I was right . . . that I must be right . . . to insist that I should be with her during her very early years.

Sometimes I even picked her up out of her cot when she was asleep, poor little mite, just for the comfort that her warm soft little body could give me. And who was being selfish then? She would open her eyes and smile sleepily at me. A pudgy hand would reach out to my face and then she would drift off again. She was such a good baby.

I trotted out all the right arguments . . . or so I thought.

'Love and security is what she needs while she is so little, Jimmy. All the time. It isn't as if either of us had any family to help out. If either of us had any brothers or sisters or my parents weren't dead and yours didn't live in

France, perhaps things might be different.'

'She'd be perfectly alright with a childminder or in a nursery. Good God, Emma, thousands of other women leave their children with someone and go out to work. Why should you be any different?'

Stung, I had retorted, 'Oh, Jimmy, it isn't like that. If we desperately needed the money then I'd have to do it. But we don't. You know we don't. I'm pretty sure that given the chance most women would prefer to stay at home with their very young children. You forget that when I used to teach I also talked a great deal to mothers.'

'Oh, of course.' His voice was sarcastic. 'You know it all, don't you. Get wise to yourself, Emma. You're just finding excuses for your selfishness. Supposing I have to get rid of the car?' he went on grimly. 'Only yesterday that twit, Bailey at the office went out of his way to inform me that he and that stuck-up wife of his are off to Spain for three weeks. We could have done even better than that if it wasn't for Je . . . for you.'

I did my best to hide my tears but I howled like a banshee when he flung out of the house in a rage, slamming the door behind him.

I heard the echo of his voice in my mind and turned over in my bed and thumped the pillow and the dragons swished their tails remorselessly. Had I been selfish, I wondered sadly. Should I have put him first? Would he still be alive now if I had?

If you're going to let your thoughts run riot, my girl, I told myself, then steer them to where you were happy. And I gave the dragons a mental kick and resolutely conjured up images of the Norfolk countryside where I had spent so many happy childhood years.

In my mind I saw the Brecklands again with their flinty fields studded with wild flowers and the narrow roadways edged with ancient twisted pines. Above all I remembered the wide translucent skies that never failed to give a feeling of freedom and space. Here, in Manchester, you never seemed to see much of the sky at all.

So strong were my memories then, that I could almost smell the fragrance of the honeysuckle and dog roses that used to run riot over the hedges bordering my beloved Aunt Maggie's garden, where I had played for most of my childhood years. I remembered the forays along the country lanes in search of blackberries. Aunt Maggie armed with a stout walking stick and I with the baskets. We would come home laden, purple-stained and a bit scratched but very pleased with ourselves. And oh, the jams she made!

I was completely wide awake by now and I sat up in bed, hugging my knees. I moved quietly, not wanting to disturb Jenny who lay, a tousled, rosy, fast asleep bundle in the camp bed beside me, the moonlight silvering her golden curls.

Home, I thought. Well, why not?

Wouldn't Jenny love it?

Memories crowded in and the germ of a resolve took hold of me and grew. I don't know how long I sat there thinking things out but at last, even more awake . . . actually, feeling more, well, alive . . . than I had for a long while, I crept out of bed, pulled on my dressing gown and, with a feeling of resolve and excitement bubbling up inside me, went quietly into the little sitting room, found pen and paper and wrote to the Norfolk Education Authority asking for a list of vacancies and an application form.

When the letter was sealed and stamped and ready in my bag for posting the next day I slipped back into bed and fell fast asleep.

The next few days were difficult. I didn't intend to tell Peggy of my decision until the reply came from the Ed. Office. I was used to telling her everything and I felt mean but I just wanted to hug the whole idea to myself for a while until I had really thought it through. When the answer to my letter arrived and I saw there was a vacancy for an Infant School teacher in a little village only a few miles from where I had spent most of my childhood, I felt as if the fates had meant this to happen and could keep quiet no longer.

I could see that Peggy found my elation hard to understand.

'I know you planned to go back to teaching just as soon as Jenny was old enough to go to school,' she said, running a hand through her hair until it stood on end. 'But for heaven's sake, why go to some god-forsaken place where you won't know anyone?'

'But I will know some people there,' I replied. 'Not everyone will have moved away.'

'Oh, Em, You can't go back in time. Face up to it, love. It must be all of eleven years since you were last in Norfolk. People you used to know will have grown up, changed, moved away, died even. You'll be disappointed and on your own.'

I can see the expression on her face now. Such a worried frown she showed me.

'I shall have Jenny. We'll be alright. Oh, Pegs, I'm convinced I'm doing the right thing. I shall miss you dreadfully but there's no-one else I shall miss or who will miss me. You know as well as I do that those so-called friends of Jimmy's never come near these days. Please try to understand. I want to give Jenny the kind of childhood that I had and I've been feeling so restless lately, knowing that I needed to give my life some kind of direction and not knowing which way to go. When I decided to go home . . . for Norfolk is home to me . . . I just knew it was the right thing to do. I've just realised that I'm a survivor and it's given me a heady sort of feeling.'

'It's gone to your head alright,' was Peggy's rather sour comment.

There the subject was shelved and tacitly ignored by both of us. I applied for the post and waited impatiently.

When the official looking letter arrived I opened it with trembling fingers, tearing the envelope in my haste. A frisson of excitement began somewhere under my ribs and trickled round and upwards towards the back of my neck. Or was it a shiver of premonition?

I wonder. If I had known that danger and anguish lay ahead of me because of this flimsy bit of paper, would I still have answered it? I think so. For if I had been given an inkling of disaster then surely I would also have been made aware of the possible joy.

Yes, it was certainly time that I took charge of my own life and started going somewhere. I had drifted for too long.

2

The letter was prosaic and very brief, merely asking me to present myself for an interview at Little Croxfield in a fortnight's time. I should have been cool, calm and collected in my new self-imposed role as a today's woman in charge of her own destiny. After all, this was no big deal . . . a post in a small country school. I was none of those things. A mixture of feelings churned in my mind as I pushed my hair back from my forehead and read the letter again. Feelings of anticipation and excitement mixed up with apprehension and, what I diagnosed afterwards, as downright cold feet.

I told Peggy this and her comment was expectedly pithy.

'I'm not surprised. I think you are utterly and completely off your trolley. Why on earth do you want to go and bury yourself in the back of beyond? Norfolk of all places. It has to be the last place God made! There'll be no theatres or concerts or good libraries or . . . decent shops or . . . or . . . or anything.' she continued vehemently. 'It's O.K. for holidays I suppose but not for full time living and surely this little tin-pot school will be a backwards step for you careerwise?'

Keyed up, I tried to explain once more my urgent longing to get away from what I thought of as the 'rat-race' of city life. To return to the tranquillity and slower pace of country living and to give my beloved Jenny the kind of childhood that I remembered with an almost painful longing.

'I'm just not sure if I'm good enough to take the job on,' I explained. 'I'm not worried about moving down to Norfolk at all.'

But Peggy battled on. 'It's just pie in the sky, Em. Just because you can dimly remember spending holidays with some old aunt you've glamourised it beyond belief. It will be muddy and messy. There'll be no public transport so you'll never be able to get anywhere. I shudder to think what the sanitation will be like. You'll have to get bathed in an old tin bath in an outhouse. You'll have to wear wellies all the time and . . . and . . . you'll get pigs in your back door and . . . straw in your hair.'

She stopped for breath, scowling but with a tell-tale twinkle in her eyes.

'Oh, Pegs. You fool.' I gave up, laughing. 'How you do exaggerate. Maybe just some of that might have been true fifty years ago but not now. Besides, I didn't just spend holidays in Norfolk. I lived there for years with my Aunt Maggie after my parents died, when I was a little girl. I obviously can't justify it to you. You are through and through a city girl. I'm not. I just feel it in my bones that it is the right move to make.'

Some of my exuberance died a quick death as a sobering thought edged into its place.

'Anyway, I haven't got the job yet.'

'You'll get it alright,' said Peggy, gloomily. 'You were one of the best teachers that Norton Primary had in a long while.'

'Well, I doubt that but thanks anyway, pal. Don't forget, Pegs that I've been away from the teaching scene for nearly five years. They might want someone with more teaching experience or even decide to give someone straight out of college a chance. I'm not counting my chickens yet.'

Feeling the need for action . . . anything to distract myself from such insidious doubts . . . I jumped up from my chair calling over my shoulder, 'Anyway, I'm starving and I'm sure you are too. Come and eat.'

I knew very well that thoughts of food would at least divert Peggy from pouncing on these doubts.

Time dragged until the day before the interview arrived. Luckily it was half-term so Peggy was at home and could look after Jenny for me. I had arranged to travel down to the centuries-old market town of Fairsham and stay overnight at the Crown, once an old coaching inn and now a comfortable hotel. Then I could present myself at the school in Little Croxfield the next morning.

I was sent off with a bear hug from Jenny who had been perfectly happy to stay behind with Peggy with a promise of a visit to a Disney film. I was filled with feeling of elation which lasted for most of the long and tedious journey. I did have one or two little niggling doubts but they were mostly concerned with finding somewhere for Jenny and I to live. But I was optimistically sure that something would turn up and as the train rat-tattled along, my resolve, along with my backbone, stiffened and I promised myself that even if I didn't get this post then I would apply for another one straight away. I'm on my way home, I told myself and let the swaying of the train send me to sleep.

At King's Lynn I had to leave the train and take a local bus. My spirits rose as I found myself listening with a secret delight to the familiar and well-loved dialect of the country wives going home from market and the old men with their sly humour and friendly calling down the bus to each other. On such a bus, although probably more rackety, my Aunt Maggie and I had travelled to Swaffham Market every Saturday.

The magnificent cock pheasants strutting across the ploughed fields in the last of the afternoon's sunshine, the winter wheat pushing up its spears of palest green, making a promise of future golden seas of corn, the flint cottages with the sun's glow on their pantiled roofs were all familiar timeless sights that conspired to lift my heart.

I leaned back against my seat, the beginnings of weariness making themselves felt . . . for it had been a long day . . . and flexed my shoulders inside the cosy wool jacket that I had bought three days ago. Pegs and Jenny and I had gone on a spending spree and I hadn't been able to resist this jacket's lovely colour and soft warmth. Pegs said the cherry red suited me and I must admit I felt good in it. There was a neat navy suit carefully folded in my case ready for the next day and Pegs had looked down her nose at it, saying it was dull but I had just grinned and said that village schoolmarms weren't supposed to look ritzy.

My eyes closed as I was lulled with the movement of the bus and to any onlookers I must have looked quiet and relaxed. No-one could have known that my innermost self was singing an almost passionate song of joy. Why had I stayed away so long, I asked myself.

At last the bus shuddered to a stop in the market square in Fairsham. I got out thankfully and the driver handed down my case with a nod and a 'There you are, my woman,' and I crossed the empty market place to the welcoming lights of the hotel. My room was comfortable and the evening meal good and I had planned to go straight to bed after it. Disconcertedly, I was now wide awake. The coffee after my meal had been rather strong and I blamed that. Seeing a bookcase in a corner of the tiny lounge I went across to rummage through it and found a Joan Dunne paperback that I hadn't read. I like her books. Her main characters . . . or heroines if you like . . . were always feisty individuals who dealt with every adversity and were always given a happy ending. Peggy scorned the books as escapism but I was always hopeful that life could be like that.

'Fate sometimes needs a little nudge,' I had once told her. Brave words but, after all, wasn't I doing just that now? If coming all this way to a new life wasn't nudging fate, then I didn't know what was. I stood a little straighter and grinned to myself. Carried along on this little wave of euphoria I did something entirely out of character and walked over to the bar. A nightcap, I thought.

I'll take it upstairs with me and perhaps it will make me sleep. Whatever I was doing I really can't imagine for I hardly ever drank. A glass of wine at Christmas was about my limit. Jimmy was always trying to get me to join him in his drinking at the parties but I never did.

Somewhere, I'm sure, Fate gave a little snicker to itself.

There were quite a few people at the bar. Probably the Crown was a popular place and I had gathered that this day had been a market day. Always a busy day in the country. I found a gap and hesitantly edged my way through. Perhaps this hadn't been such a good idea after all. I stood for a moment feeling a bit out of place and then turned to go and retrieve the book I had left on a table. At the same moment a man who had been standing at my side grabbed my shoulder and swung me back again.

His red face and glassy eyes told their own tale and I tried to pull away.

'Come you on, m'dear, I'll soon get

you served.' He called to the barman. 'Jack, this here li'l lady wants a drink. Stir yourself.'

Several people turned round for his voice was loud and hectoring and I was most horribly embarrassed.

'No. really. Thank you . . . it's alright. I was just going.'

But before I could wriggle out of his grasp he had thrust a drink into my hand and I was obliged to take it or suffer the consequences of it going all the way down the front of my dress. At the same time someone behind me jogged my arm and the contents of my glass flew up in the air and cascaded all the way down a rather nice tweed jacket that was just in front of my nose.

Horrified, I looked up at its wearer and encountered a pair of the bluest eyes I had ever seen. Definitely not sunny, blue sky sort of eyes. No way. Without doubt. These were dark and stormy.

I could have sworn that he looked at me as if he recognised me . . . and wasn't pleased about it. Then the moment passed . . . It could only have been for seconds that I stared up at this man and yet it felt like forever and for some unexplainable reason I felt a weird little frisson start at the back of my neck and trickle down my back. Then he pulled out a handkerchief and began to mop himself, glaring at me.

'Oh, I am so sorry.' I apologised. 'Someone knocked me and . . . '

'Don't worry.' he said, curtly. 'It'll dry.' But it was said without a vestige of a smile and his gaze raked me up and down. I wished that I could sink into the ground. Even more so when that tipsy man flung his arm round my shoulder and roared with laughter.

'Don't you worry, my woman. Ol' Jimma'll soon get you another.'

That you won't, I thought and squeezed my way out of the crush, grabbed up my book and fled, hoping I might never look into those dark blue eyes again.

So why was it that when I had turned

off my light and resolutely snuggled under my blankets I could see that uncompromising expression so clearly in my mind's eye? . . . and the way his dark unruly hair flopped over his forehead . . . and . . . I turned over and thumped my pillow and turned my thoughts to what the next day would bring.

The next day brought most unseasonably bright sunshine and blue skies and I thought happily about the spring which would soon be here. My high spirits lasted until after breakfast and then, unaccountably, sank like a pricked balloon. Now that the actual day of my interview had arrived I was suddenly beset with all sorts of doubts. What was I doing here, I thought wildly. Supposing Peggy was right and I was being foolhardy to come back to Norfolk so far away from the place I had lived in for the last eight years or so. I did have a few friends there after all and maybe I would find everything changed down here. What about living accomodation?

How would I manage? As these and other questions filled my mind, for a few irrational moments I contemplated flight. Turning about and beating a hasty retreat to Manchester. Then the hotel receptionist came to tell me that the taxi I had ordered to drive me the few miles to Little Croxfield was waiting in the square . . . and common sense prevailed.

I gritted my teeth, squared my shoulders and glared at myself in the mirror.

'Wimp!' I said out loud and fastened the last button of my jacket very firmly. My navy suit looked trim and smart and although my shoulder length blonde hair was loose and curly it looked glossy enough. I had tried to put it up earlier thinking it might look better but after two desperate attempts I had finally given up and let it go its own way. Slinging my bag over my shoulder, I gave it a pat and went out into the sunny morning. I made myself smile at the receptionist, said good morning to the taxi driver and slid into the seat next to him, feeling as if I was going to my execution.

I had chosen to sit next to him thinking he would be a local man and could perhaps talk to me about places and people that I used to know but he proved to be a newcomer and couldn't answer my eager questions, so I gave up and contented myself with looking around at the passing countryside. The part of Norfolk where I had lived as a little girl was further away than I had thought, on the other side of Fairsham so I didn't know this particular area and yet it all seemed so familiar. In what seemed like no time at all we arrived at my destination and pulled up outside the school and the driver promised to return for me in two hours time.

I pushed the gate open slowly, the sun-bleached wood rough under my hand, reminding me of just such another one. A smaller gate that had opened into the flower-filled garden of my Aunt Maggie's cottage. I looked across the asphalt playground to the small red-brick building and it was as if I had come home. All my doubts and uncertainties disappeared as if they had never been and I remember how eagerly I looked round.

The little school had a friendly air and certainly the facilities were good. A large playing field to the left contained a football pitch, a slide and swings. A climbing frame, shiny with much use, stood sturdily in one corner of the playground and, in another corner on a rather worn patch of grass and sheltered by a large privet bush I saw two roomy rabbit hutches. Their occupants, two placid contented-looking white rabbits, lay stretched out by the wire netting sunning themselves.

'Oh, you beauties,' I breathed. 'My Jenny would love you.'

My little Jenny who adored anything furry and on four legs and who continually begged for a puppy or a kitten. An impossible request, living as we did in someone else's house.

I walked slowly up to the school door taking in the date of 1882 carved into the stonework above it and, as I reached out my hand to grasp the door handle it turned, making me jump and the door opened to frame a large untidy-looking man with a shock of greying hair.

'Mrs. Dane?' he asked.

I gulped and nodded and managed a nervous smile but he responded with one of such singular kindness that I relaxed and stepped into the small porch with slightly more confidence.

'I'm Douglas Rawdon, the head-master.' he said and held out his hand. 'Do come in, Mrs, Dane.'

Ushering me in to what was obviously the Reception classroom with its walls displaying colourful splodges of paintings and its corners full of toys, he introduced me to two other women sitting on chairs by the side of one of the child-sized tables. They were just about to help themselves from a tray of coffee.

'Make yourself comfortable, Mrs. Dane and have a cup of coffee. We're nearly ready to start the interviews.' He grinned again. 'There's always someone who keeps you waiting . . . but don't worry,' he added hastily, 'I wasn't referring to you.'

Peggy always said that anyone could read my face like an open book and he must have seen the dismay that I felt at his words.

At that moment, a distant door banged and we could hear a rather strident female voice coming from the next room. Mr. Rawdon pushed a large hand through his already tousled hair and with an 'Excuse me, ladies,' disappeared in its direction.

I sat down, reached for a sorely needed cup of coffee and peeked over its rim at my companions. After some desultory conversation I soon realised that these two candidates probably had more to offer than I did. One, I guessed was just a few months out of college. A thin, lanky girl, she had an air of supreme self assurance and I could imagine she was no doubt bursting with all the latest educational theories. Very wrong of me, I daresay but I hated her on sight. The other, a more mature lady, had a motherly manner and obviously a wealth of experience.

I was the last one to be interviewed and, as the other applicants came out of the next room in turn, my confidence oozed away. The younger woman bounced out with such a complacent look on her face that I found myself gripping my bag quite painfully. As the older woman was called in I turned and made myself ask with a casual air that I was far from feeling,

'How did it go then? Are there many people in there?'

'Oh, it went brilliantly.' she gave a small snort of laughter. 'After all, it does help to know all the latest methods,' adding, with a disparaging look around her, 'although I daresay they would be wasted on a place like this. I have to say that although this Mr.

Rawdon seems decent enough he does seem to be a bit behind the times.'

She brushed an imaginary speck from the lapel of her immaculate jacket and sat a little straighter.

'It will be quite a challenge. Oh, there's only five of them in there. Nothing to it.'

I felt my hackles rise and itched to wipe the smug smile off her face. I don't know what had got into me. I wasn't usually so intolerant. But perhaps it was because I had loved the look of this little school and I quite desperately wanted to get the job. When the older woman returned, also smiling confidently, my spurt of disapproval sank and my heart went with it. Dismayingly, I began to shake.

I reminded myself that I was no longer an untried girl and that the last ten years had taught me well . . . about all sorts of things. Now was the time to put that teaching into practice. I would be calm and serene and let no-one guess that inside my absolutely composed bearing I was shaking like a leaf blown in the wind and my one desire was to be done with the whole business and head for home.

Did the fates see inside my head and chuckle again at what was in store for me?

As Mr. Rawdon ushered me in I rallied myself and, thankfully, what followed was nothing like as daunting as I had feared.

Except for one thing.

Mr. Rawdon took care to put me at my ease as he introduced me to the other members of the committee. Sitting facing me was the Vicar, an elderly man fighting a losing battle with his sparse grey hair and who had a most beguiling look of innocence on his chubby features. Next to him was a plump young woman of about my own age and introduced as Pat Somers, the member from the P.T.A. She shook my hand warmly, giving me a wide and friendly smile. Another older woman with a lean intelligent face sat at the side of the heavy battle-scarred desk.

'Parish Council,' she said, briskly. 'Glad to meet you m'dear.'

They were so kind and welcoming that I relaxed, feeling completely at ease and ready to answer any questions they might ask.

I turned to meet the final member, sitting at the other end of Mr. Rawdon's desk and can well remember my reaction.

I had gazed into those dark blue eyes before. This time they were even more hostile.

This was so unexpected that, for what could only have been a nanosecond and yet felt like eternity, I was aware of shock ripping through me. The shock of some kind of recognition. Yet how could that be? Discounting our brief meeting of the previous evening, I knew I had never set eyes on this man at any time of my life. I would certainly not have forgotten. I felt myself blink and the moment was gone.

I had noticed that he was tall in that crush in the bar. Now I could see that he was also broad-shouldered with the physique of an athlete, giving out the impression of controlled strength. Definitely the most good-looking man I had seen in a long while although his features were more rugged than classical. Yet what had registered with me overwhelmingly at that first glance was the expression on his face.

His eyes were narrowed and his mouth a tight straight line. Those good looks were marred by fierce, unmistakeable disapproval . . . and it was directed straight at me.

Mr. Rawdon was speaking but I only vaguely heard his words.

'This is Andrew Bruce, our local Veterinary Surgeon, and one of our school governors as well. Busy as he undoubtedly is, he has found time to come here today. For which, many thanks Andrew.'

I automatically held out my hand, looking up as I did so to encounter those vivid dark blue eyes that held no warmth at all. He took my hand for a second and then dropped it as if it had been a red hot coal. It was this rather ungracious act that brought me to my senses. I turned, a shade desperately, to Mr. Rawdon. What have I done? I thought wildly. Why on earth should that man look at me like that? As if he hates me. I only spilt a bit of gin down his jacket for goodness sake.

I could see the tiniest frown of puzzlement on the headmaster's face as he glanced from those forbidding features to mine, which I felt sure were betraying me. Then he launched smoothly into questions about my background and experience and the difficult moment was passed over.

Towards the end of the interview, I allowed myself another quick look at Andrew Bruce, to see him leaning back in his chair with his arms folded across his chest, surveying me with a shuttered expression, his body language proclaiming antagonism, loud and clear.

For a moment I thought a small draught had blown across my back and then I realised, with something approaching horror, that the small hairs on the back of my neck were standing on end.

Never before had any part of me had such an instinctive and uncontrollable reaction to another person.

3

I took a deep breath and turned away from the hostility which reached out to me from Andrew Bruce and concentrated on answering the questions from the other committee members seated at the desk. There was an anger in me, strangely enough, directed at myself. Not so long ago I had promised myself that never again was I going to let any man browbeat or intimidate me. I was not about to give up on that promise now. In an odd sort of way that spurt of anger was just what I needed and when I looked back on that interview as I was travelling home, I felt sure it had gone well. I'd given a good account of myself anyway and that was all that mattered just then. I wouldn't know whether or not I had been successful until later.

Once home and with Jenny tucked up in bed, Peggy bombarded me with questions, wanting to know every detail and I did my best to satisfy her.

'To be honest, Pegs, the interview all seems a bit of a blur now,' I eventually said. 'I can't remember what they asked or what I answered. I just hope I didn't make a complete fool of myself.'

'Oh, rubbish. You'll not have done that, Em. Cheer up, You'll soon know one way or the other.'

'One question sticks in my mind though. I was asked if I would miss all the night life of the city. What a thing to ask! As if that had anything to do with teaching. Stupid man!'

She gave me a very quizzical look then and leaned back in her chair, folding her arms.

'Oh oh. Who rattled your cage then? Come on, give. You've got a shifty look about you and I want to get to the bottom of it,' and she pressed her lips together in mock severity.

'Oh, Pegs, you fool. We . . e . . ll, there was something that was a bit weird.'

'I knew it,' she crowed and sat forward. 'Well . . . ?'

So I told her of the puzzling reaction of a certain member of the interviewing committee and, as I spoke, a picture crept slyly into my mind of cold forbidding features, dark unruly hair falling over a tanned forehead and piercing blue eyes. With a little jolt, I realised that while I had spoken the truth about the interview being such a blur, I could recall every line, every facet of that handsome angry face with the utmost clarity.

I ran my fingers through my hair, brushing it back from my face.

'I just can't understand it. He hardly asked me any questions at all.'

Peggy looked at me and grinned then.

'Well, he certainly seems to have made an impression, this Mr. High-and Mighty, judging by your face. Was he so devastating?'

'Certainly not,' I said shortly. 'He'd just made up his mind about me from the start.' And I told her then about the small catastrophe of the previous evening.

'Perhaps he'd set his heart on one of the other candidates. I don't know, and you can take that grin off your face because I don't care, either.' But I grinned back at her as I went into the kitchen to make a bedtime drink.

I had so convinced myself that it would all come to nothing that when a letter arrived offering me the post of assistant teacher at Little Croxfield Primary School, I could hardly take it in at first. Then I gave a whoop of joy and scooped up my little Jenny in a bear hug.

'Jenny, Oh, Jenny. We're going to live in the country. In Norfolk, where Mummy used to live when she was a little girl.'

I waltzed round the room with her in my arms, babbling away about it all.

'You'll love it. There are fluffy white rabbits at the school and we shall have our own little house and' . . . rashly throwing all caution to the winds . . . 'You shall have your puppy . . . perhaps a kitten too.'

Jenny's eyes widened and two plump little arms nearly strangled me.

'Ooh, Mummy, really?'

We collapsed, laughing, in the arm-chair and I hugged Jenny to me and told her of the new life that was opening up before us.

'What about the little house, Mummy? What's it like?'

'Well, love, I haven't seen it properly yet so I can't tell you. As far as I can remember it is built of old red brick like the school and it is just next door, so we won't have far to go to school, will we?'

That indeed had been a bonus, for in the letter from the Education Office had been a postscript to the effect that the school house at Little Croxfield was vacant and had been for some time as Mr. Rawdon had bought property in a neighbouring village. Would I like to rent it for the time being? Would I! Everything seemed to be falling into place and I could hardly believe my good luck.

I wasted no time, but sat down that morning to reply, accepting the post and thanking them for the offer of the school house. I also wrote that I would be able to start work after the Easter holidays as they wanted. Wrapped up warmly against the chill January wind, Jenny and I went off to post my letter, Jenny demanding to be lifted up so that she could pop it carefully into the letter box.

Then, beaming all over her rosy little face, she turned and said,

'Now can we go and get my puppy?'

I wished, ruefully, that I had had the sense to keep quiet about a puppy and it took all the length of the journey home to explain to a downcast little girl just why she would have to wait for a little while longer.

There followed a time of frenzied activity.

'I can't believe it's taking so long to pack,' I said to Peggy one Saturday morning. 'Where has all this stuff come from?'

'Well, you'll certainly need all these bits and pieces I've been storing for you. Aren't you glad you saved them now?'

Peggy was as dusty as I was sure I was, from going up into her loft.

'It will be rather fun, setting up house again, won't it? What are you going to do about furniture?'

'Fairsham is quite a good sized market town and I should be able to get what I want there. If not, then Norwich isn't far away and there are some lovely shops there. That's why I'm going down early.'

I thought of the stylish pieces I used to own and sighed regretfully.

'You know there was no way I could have kept the things I used to have, once the house was sold. Never mind, as you say, it will be fun, choosing furniture and planning colour schemes, especially as I can do it all exactly as I want to.' I chuckled and added, 'If I want to paint the kitchen pink with purple spots, I can ... and there's no-one to stop me.'

The chuckle turned into a giggle as the look of disbelief on Peggy's face.

'It's alright, Pegs. I promise I won't go that far. But it will be nice to please myself ... as far as funds permit, of course.' I thought of my last bank statement and pulled a wry face at my friend.

'I should think that the money I have left over from the sale of the house will just about cover it all ... and keep us in bread and jam until my first pay-day comes along. I would have had more if it hadn't been for that hefty mortgage.'

'If you want to ...' began Peggy but I forestalled her on that one, knowing full well what was in her generous mind.

'No, Pegs. I know what you're going to say and thank you, but no. Don't worry. We shall be fine.'

'If you're sure ... just remember that I'm here for you. One good thing, weren't you lucky with that little school house?'

'Oh, yes. Although, remember that I only saw it from outside. Mr. Rawdon did say, in that letter he sent me last week, that it would need some redecorating, although the building is sound enough. He said that various people have rented it since he had it, so goodness knows what sort of a state it will be in. He's fixed us up with a Mrs. Parfitt in the village. She's going to put us up for a couple of weeks or so until I get the place cleaned and decorated.'

I stuffed some more of my newspaper-wrapped china into the cardboard box in front of me and fastened the lid.

'You know, Pegs, I'm really looking forward to it.' I sat back on my heels and gave a happy sigh. I felt so optimistic and . . . well . . . lively, I suppose. I looked across at Peggy and cursed myself for she was looking down at her hands and her face was sad. I leaned across and took her hands in mine, feeling a lump in my throat.

'Pegs, I'm sorry to leave you. That is my only regret. You've been such a good friend to us both. I . . . I . . . wouldn't have survived without you.'

She looked up and grinned, the sadness wiped away in a second.

'What rot. Of course you would. You're a fighter, girl and don't you forget it. I shall miss you both . . . and I shall miss your cooking.' She patted her slightly ample curves. 'Maybe I shall be able to lose a bit of weight at last. It always annoyed me to death that although you ate the same as I did you never put weight on. Look at you now. A figure that makes me want to spit spiders.'

Jenny was under the table, busily wrapping her toys in dozens of sheets of newspaper and she crawled out and looked up at Peggy with such horror that we both burst out laughing and the moment of emotion was safely passed.

I stood up and stretched.

'There, that's nearly the last of the boxes done. Don't forget, Pegs, you've promised to come down and stay during the Easter holidays. Hopefully I should have most of the house decorated and furnished by then.'

'Talk about optimism!' Peggy chuckled. 'I'm looking forward to it, pal. In fact, wild horses wouldn't keep me away.' She heaved a doleful sigh. 'I suppose I shall have to buy a pair of wellies.'

I flapped a dismissive hand at her and she went on.

'I still think you're mad. You could just as easily have done all this nearer home.'

I sat down again and spoke to her as earnestly as I could, for I did so want her to understand.

'Pegs, you must realise that Norfolk is home to me. You can't imagine how I felt when I went down there for that interview. O.K. so what if people I used to know have moved away or forgotten me. I shall soon make new friends. It would be more like home if Aunt Maggie was still around,' and, for a moment, the old familiar sadness caused me to falter and I couldn't stop a sigh from welling up. 'But . . . but even so, it's my place, It's where I belong.'

'She was your mother's sister, wasn't she?' asked Peggy, curiously.

'Mm, yes, but she was years older than Mum. She was such a lovely person. When my parents were killed in that plane crash, she came straight over to take me to live with her. I was only five at the time.' I glanced over to my own small daughter, who was now importantly stuffing her ill-wrapped parcels into a large cardboard box.

'Not much older than Jenny. It must have been a big decision for her to take on such a small child at the drop of a hat. Especially as she had always been on her own until then and was used to her own ways. I don't remember a great deal about those early days with her but I do know that I soon grew to love her and was happy. I had a good life with her. I went to the village school at first. A little place very like the one at

Croxford. Then on to the Grammar School at Swaffham. I used to cycle the five miles to school every day and back again, hail, rain or shine.'

I looked up and laughed.

'You were right, in a way, with your disparaging remarks about public transport. There was no school bus for me.' I chuckled again, remembering. 'You should have seen my first bike. I think Aunt Maggie paid a fiver for it at Swaffham market. It was a real bone-shaker. Then she bought me a new Raleigh for my birthday. My word! How I fancied myself then.'

There was a look of disbelief spreading across Peggy's face that was almost comical.

'Oh, Pegs, you should see your face.'

'Well. Can you wonder? I mean . . . cycling in all weathers, ten miles a day. You poor little brat.' She shivered dramatically. 'Didn't you hate it?'

'No-oo. I used to fly like a bird.'

Keeping a straight face, I clapped my hands together.

'Why, I've just had a brilliant idea. I might get Jenny and myself bikes, when we've been down a while and I could hire one for you when you come to visit.' At the dawning look of horror on Peggy's face I collapsed into laughter.

'Don't worry, pal. Just testing.'

'Thank God for that. For a minute there I thought you were serious.'

I wrapped up a few more plates, amusement still lurking.

'It was a good life, you know. Aunt Maggie gave me such security and love. She was a very clever woman and a brilliant naturalist. I suppose my love of the countryside stems from her teaching. She wrote several books on the subject.'

'Did she now? I didn't know that. I don't think you've ever mentioned that before. I apologise for calling her 'some old aunt' the other day.'

'I've got all her books somewhere. I think they're packed away with the others now. I thought I'd shown them to you.'

Peggy shook her head and then I painfully remembered why.

'No, come to think of it, you wouldn't have seen them. I packed them away up into our loft years ago.'

I bent my head, my hands busy again, remembering Jimmy's acid remarks when I had proudly put my aunt's books on display. Horrified at his accusation of showing off, I had put them out of sight to please him. How spineless I had been. Why on earth had I been such a wimp? No wonder he got fed up with me. It would probably have been better if I had stood up to him a bit more. Thinking that I had done everything wrong, I sighed dispiritedly. Peggy must have heard me and guessed that my thoughts then were not exactly happy ones, for she spoke quickly.

'I expect she was quite a celebrity in your village.'

'Yes. Yes she probably was. She was certainly a character and spoke her mind.' I felt my eyes misting. 'I do wish she'd lived longer. I would have liked her to know about Jenny. She died, you know, just before I came out of training college.' I heaved another sigh and added quietly, 'Anyway, she never knew about Jimmy's accident either so that was a blessing.'

I looked across at Peggy then and guessed from the grim expression on her face that she was sharing my thought that it was also as well that my dear old aunt had never known of my grief and heartache.

When I had finally packed all my belongings, I realised that I would only need a small van to transport them down to Little Croxfield and I opted to travel down in the van with them. I soon regretted this decision for the journey was long and tiring and the weather was bad. We even had to push our way through a bit of a blizzard at one stage. I cuddled Jenny up to me and gazed at the sleet trickling down the windscreen gloomily. The van driver was taciturn and, to my mind, on a par with the weather. The van seats were uncomfortable and various hold-ups on the way meant that we arrived at the school house much later than scheduled. All my possessions were quickly unloaded and piled into the cold little sitting room and I was too tired and weary to protest overmuch at the removal man's careless handling of my things and just glad to pay him off and see the back of him.

By then the dusk had deepened into darkness but when I wandered into the kitchen and pressed the light switch it brought no result. Obviously my letter asking for the power to be re-connected had not been attended to.

A small cold hand tugged at my arm. 'Mummy, I'm tired.' quavered an equally small voice.

I hoisted Jenny up into my arms with a swift hug and a kiss.

'Never mind, poppet. We'll lock up and go and find this Mrs. Parfitt's house and then we'll soon be all warm and cosy. We'll see to all this in the morning.'

'I don't like it being dark,' wailed Jenny and buried her face in my neck, stifling a sob.

As I was feeling very much the same, I almost shrieked aloud when the door opened behind me with a protesting and eerie groan.

'Come you on, my dears,' said a warm, countrified voice. 'You don't want to stay in this cold place now. I thought I saw that there removals van arrive. I've a'bin watching out for it for long enough. You'll be Mrs. Dane then?'

I turned to see a plump little figure filling the kitchen doorway, the light from a wavering torch casting a faint glow on the rosy face above it.

'I'm Mrs. Parfitt and it's only a step across the road to my house. You just pick up what you want for tonight and I'll take the little girl.'

She held out a hand and I put Jenny down and thankfully reached for our overnight bag.

'We're so glad to see you, Mrs.

Parfitt. I was just coming to find you. There's no electricity on.'

'If that 'ent just like them,' was the cryptic response. 'Well, they'll come when they're ready, no doubt. Come you on my little darlin' and we'll soon have you right as nine pence.'

Jenny went willingly with such a comfortable little person and I locked the door behind us and followed them down the gravel path and along the village street to a near-by brick and flint cottage. A flickering orange glow from the window told of a welcoming fire and soon we were feeling its warmth and Mrs. Parfitt wasted no time before seating us at the table with plates of appetising beef stew and dumplings in front of us.

'Now them's proper Norfick dumplings.' She nodded her head encouragingly at Jenny. 'My Harbert, God rest his soul, allus enjoyed them.'

'Is he going to come and have some with us?' enquired Jenny, looking round interestedly.

A shadow passed over Mrs. Parfitt's cheerful face as she answered soberly.

'No, my darlin'. Harbert 'ent with us any longer. He's in Heaven now.'

Embarassed, I apologised.

'I'm so sorry, Mrs. Parfitt. Jenny, love. Eat your supper.'

'Why, bless us, my dear. Thass alright.' The little woman beamed at me. 'Thass just the sort of thing a child would ask. My Harbert's been gone a few years now . . . and time does heal you know.'

She leaned across the table and patted my hand.

'Now just you remember that.'

Ruefully, I realised that she and no doubt most other people in the village knew quite a bit about me by now. I well remembered village life and the interest which was always shown towards newcomers.

Jenny was practically falling asleep over her plate so we soon had her tucked up in the big double bed that she was to share with me and I felt so exhausted that I was sure that I wouldn't be far behind her. Mrs. Parfitt apologised for not having another room to spare but I assured her that we would do splendidly. The low-ceilinged room was spotlessly clean and the pink flowered curtains and matching bed-spread gave it a warm cosy feeling. As I slid quietly into bed that night I was very glad of the warm little body snuggling up to me and I fell into a dreamless sleep almost before my head touched the pillow.

The next morning dawned bright and clear and the first thing I wanted to do was to go and explore my new home and put it into some sort of order.

'We'll give Auntie Pegs a ring tonight,' I told Jenny as we walked hand in hand up the village street. 'Just to let her know that we've arrived safely.'

I paused with my hand on the gate. The school house stood four-square and sturdy, the mellowed brick rosy in the spring sunshine. Maybe I was being fanciful but it seemed to welcome me and, with a sigh of pure pleasure, I lifted the old-fashioned latch and we made our way up the path. The front garden was a mess. There was no other word for it. Weeds rioted through the rank grass of what had once been a patch of lawn and brambles reached out to us with thorny fingers that spread far and wide from the encircling hedge.

'Later,' I promised it, with what I hoped was a militant look, ' . . . and I shall look forward to it.'

Once inside, Jenny ran from room to room and up the steep flight of stairs that led from a narrow hallway.

'Which is my room, Mummy? Can I have this one with the big cupboard in? Look at me. I can get right in.' She peered out from the white painted doorway, giggling.

'That room will be just right for you, love. You'll be able to keep all your toys in that lovely big cupboard, won't you?'

I stepped into the front bedroom and

gave a gasp of dismay mixed with amusement.

'Oh, my God! Come and look at this, Jenny.'

'Yuk!' was Jenny's comment and, 'Yuk, indeed,' I echoed, with a giggle. For the room was enough to give anyone a bilious attack. It had been papered with three different patterns of wallpaper, all in shades of acid and olive green. Stripes and swirls completed the nauseous effect.

This is definitely going to be my first job, I decided and, finding pencil and paper, went over the house from top to bottom, making a list of what was necessary. Fortunately the tiny bathroom was in good repair, only crying out for a good scrub but the other two bedrooms and the sitting room really needed a face lift.

'Mrs. Parfitt told me that it's market day in Fairsham tomorrow, Jenny. We can go in on the market bus and get all the decorating things and then I shall have to get my sleeves rolled up.'

'What are you going to do?' asked Jenny, curiously.

'Paint all the woodwork . . . you know, the doors and window frames . . . and put some pretty paper on the walls.'

I spoke with more confidence that I actually felt. I'd never done any decorating before but I couldn't see why it should be all that difficult. Aunt Maggie had always done her own. I remembered she had always let me mix the wallpaper paste but that was as far as my expertise went.

'And what's market day?'

'I was forgetting. You've never been to a country market. I think you'll find it great fun. Come on, sweetheart, we'll go to the village shop to buy cleaning things and I'll tell you all about market days when I was a little girl like you. I remember once there was a man with a barrel organ and he had a little monkey . . . .'

During the next two weeks I worked my way steadily through that little house, scrubbing and cleaning, painting and papering. My initial attempts at paper-hanging were a bit disastrous and I think I got more paint on myself than on the window frames but I learned the hard way and gradually improved, feeling terrifically proud of myself when the first room was finished. I had found ample choice in Fairsham when looking for furnishings and had thoroughly enjoyed myself choosing materials in soft misty shades of blue and green to harmonise with the glowing golden pine furniture I had found in the one large store in the town. When I had demolished the terrible décor in what was to be my bedroom, painted the woodwork a soft creamy white and covered the walls with the prettiest of yellow flowered wallpaper, the room felt full of sunshine even on the dullest day.

Jenny had chosen the wallpaper for her own room and although the riot of pink cabbage roses was not exactly my choice, she was very happy with it and that was the main thing. A plain green carpet toned it down a bit and she said it would be like sleeping in a garden. That said it all.

'I'm having such fun, Pegs,' I told my friend over the phone, one evening. 'I never knew I could do all this. Oh, I daresay some of the wallpaper doesn't hang dead straight in the corners and if you look for brush-marks in the paintwork you'll find them but, on the whole, it's not too bad. I'm dying for you to come down and see it all.'

'Another two weeks and I'll be there,' she promised. 'I have to say that you sound on top of the world, Em. I'm so pleased.'

My phone had only been installed that day and I had been putting the finishing touches to the narrow hallway. As I walked towards the front door, I straightened the mirror on the wall and peered at myself. Well, I am happy, I thought with a touch of surprise and I really do look fit. My hair, which I liked to think was my best feature, being golden blonde and with a natural curl in it, seemed to have more curl than usual and certainly more shine . . . even when daubed with splashes of white paint. The pale face I had been presenting to the world during the last year had developed more colour and my eyes were clearer. I confess to preening myself a little and giving myself an extra wide smile. 'Not bad for an old lady of twenty eight,' I told my reflection and then huffed at myself and put my hand to my mouth with a giggle, glad that Jenny was not about.

While I had been so busy, Jenny had explored the overgrown garden, ventured into the school playground while the bigger children were at their lessons and fallen in love with the white rabbits.

'Oh, Mummy,' she had sighed blissfully. 'You should just see how their little pink noses nibble up and down when I poke a piece of grass through the wire for them.'

'Noses don't nibble, darling.' I spoke abstractedly as I was concentrating on persuading the last piece of dainty flower-sprigged wallpaper into place in the smallest bedroom, which was about to become my guest room.

'Theirs do,' was Jenny's firm rejoinder as she skipped off down the steep stairway. Hesitating at the bottom, she turned and called up to me.

'Mummy, when are we going to get my puppy? You did promise.'

I smiled ruefully at the reproach in her voice and thought quickly.

'Well, love, we must wait until we move in here and we can't do that until I have finished all the decorating and moved the furniture in. We've got to have beds to sleep in at least. But it won't be long now. I tell you what. We'll wait until Auntie Pegs comes and then she can help us look for one. Will that do?'

She heaved an exaggerated sigh. 'I s'pose so.'

The next evening, when Jenny had been tucked up in bed and Mrs. Parfitt and I were sitting companionably in front of the fire, I brought up the subject of a puppy.

'Where do you think I might get one from, Mrs. Parfitt? I don't want a pedigree or anything like that but I'm not too keen on pet shops.'

'No, my dear, nor do you want to be. Oh, I grant you some are good but you'd do much better getting one from the place where it's bin bred. Let me think now. Ol' Billy Williamson's Bess had pups a short while back but I do think they may be all gone by now.'

She thought a little longer and then he face brightened.

'I know. Whyever didn't I think on it a 'fore? You go along to young Mr. Bruce. He knows of all the bitches in whelp in these here parts. He'll be able to put you in the way of getting a nice little pup for my lady upstairs.'

She beamed and nodded her head knowingly.

'If she's told me once, she's told me a hundred times that she's going to have a puppy.'

I sighed. 'I feel as if everything is happening at once. I do hope that I'm doing the right thing in getting a dog so soon. But I did promise Jenny.'

'Never break a promise. Especially to a child. Thass what I say. Anyway, you'll have time to settle it in and housetrain it a bit a 'fore you start school.'

'What an optimist!' I gave a mock groan and we both laughed.

'This Mr. Bruce,' I asked. 'Who is he? Is he someone who lives in the village?'

'Why, he's the Vet, Mrs. Dane. Lives in that big old house at the end of the street. You must have met him, surely. He's one of the school governors.'

For some peculiar reason I suddenly felt short of breath and my cheeks felt hot. Now I remembered . . . only too well. Lulled by the cosy atmosphere in the little sitting room, the name hadn't registered at first. The memory of vivid blue eyes studying me from behind that desk and that angry set face, flashed into my mind and caused a shiver to ripple across my shoulders. With utter disbelief, I felt a strange little spiral of heat deep inside myself. It shocked me, this blind, involuntary response to the thought of a man who had been so obviously hostile. Horrified at myself and flustered, I shivered again.

'Are you feeling a draught, my dear?' enquired a kindly Mrs. Parfitt.

'No, no . . . of course not. It's lovely and warm in here.'

I pulled myself together and forced a laugh.

'It . . . it was nothing. Just a shiver. A . . . a goose walked over my grave! Isn't that what they say?' Then, in what I hoped was a brisk and cheerful voice, I added, 'This Mr. Bruce, won't he mind me bothering him? Vets are busy people.'

'Bless you, no. He won't mind at all. He'll be only too pleased. He's often looking for homes for unwanted pups. Can't abide putting any young creature down.'

I thought wryly of his apparent

attitude towards me and wondered if he was one of those people who prefer animals to human beings. But I wasn't about to discuss him with Mrs. Parfitt. In fact, I thought, gritting my teeth, I didn't even want to think about the wretched man again, full stop. So I made some non-committal response to the little woman and if that lady noticed my lack of enthusiasm she made no comment. However, she wasn't about to let this opportunity for a bit of village gossip slip by her and settled herself more comfortably into her chair. I already knew her well enough to recognise the signs.

'That Andrew Bruce now,' she began, 'He's a real nice young man. It was such a pity about him.' She paused and looked at me expectantly but I refused to rise to the bait, merely leaning forward to hold my hands to the fire. Undeterred, she carried on.

'He was engaged and everything and then, just before the wedding, his intended upped and ran off with her boss.'

She leaned back in her chair and pulled in her chin, disapprovingly. I did look up then and she took that as a signal to tell me more.

'She allus was a flighty piece, that Margaret Allingham, from what I heard tell . . . and had an eye to the main chance. She worked for Anglia television in Norwich and this man she run off with was very well off. A lot older than her, mind but I don't suppose she cared about that. I heard they used to go out drinking and dancing and all that. They do say her parents haven't heard from her since.'

She heaved a gusty sigh and shook her head.

'Eh dear. There are times when I think it's just as well that Harbert and I never had any young 'uns.'

So that's it, I thought. The man has obviously become a woman hater. I felt a twinge of disappointment at what I could only see as immaturity. If everyone who was disappointed in love fell into the trap of hating the opposite sex, where on earth would we all be?

But I was a little way off the mark.

Mrs. Parfitt put her head on one side and looked at me intently.

'You know, Mrs. Dane, I got quite a shock when I first saw you.'

I sat up in my chair and my mouth must have fallen open in surprise, for she laughed gently.

'You're so like Margaret. To look at, that is. Oh, no, you're not the same kind of person at all. I can tell that,' and she nodded wisely. 'But she was a real pretty girl with lovely blonde hair just like you. I tell you, at first glance you could be her double.'

Peggy always said I had a tell-tale face for Mrs. Parfitt added hastily, 'Only at first glance mind you. That one always looked discontented to my way of thinking and that spoiled her pretty looks.'

I got up from my chair and remarked as casually as I could that it was often said that everyone has a double somewhere, adding that it was time that I was off to bed.

'You go and see Mr. Bruce,' she called after me. 'Like I said, he'll be sure to find you a nice little pup.'

But I pretended not to hear and hurried up the stairs, seething. I am sure that no-one likes to be thought of as a carbon copy and I had absolutely no intention of tangling with that bad tempered self-opinionated man. 'If I ever do,' I muttered to myself as I pulled my clothes off, 'I'll make sure he gets a real set down.'

I was to remember those fighting thoughts with a certain amount of chagrin in days to come.

As I slid quietly into bed I told myself that I probably wouldn't ever need to meet him again. Our paths would never cross . . . and a good job too. I thumped my pillow with unnecessary force and Jenny turned over and murmured in her sleep. Stupid woman, I castigated myself, stop it. Although what I was supposed to stop I didn't think too closely about.

As luck would have it, my path crossed Andrew Bruce's the very next day and with disastrous results.

I had left Jenny with Mrs. Parfitt for the morning. She was going to help that lady with the baking, I was told, and as I was putting the finishing touches to some paintwork I didn't try too hard to persuade her otherwise. During the morning I looked round for some white spirit to clean my brushes with and then remembered that I had used it all the previous day. There was no problem, for the village shop, like most of its kind, stocked just about every-thing from paraffin to peas. I only had to dash across the road. I noticed, thankfully, that the street was deserted, for I wasn't at my tidiest. I had tied my hair up in a ponytail with a frayed old scarf and was wearing an ancient pair of cut-off jeans and a sweat shirt, both of which were liberally splashed with paint. Mrs. Colley at the shop was used to seeing me like this by now as I often popped in for cleaning materials and snacks.

Once in the shop, I picked up the white spirit and a packet of washing powder and had just put my purse back in my pocket when Mrs. Colley reached under the counter and fetched out a large paint tin.

'Could you use this, Mrs. Dane?' she asked. 'I've had it left over from my last lot of decorating and I know I shan't use it now. I'm sure you have a lot to do over there and it's a real pretty colour.'

'Why, thank you, Mrs. Colley. That is kind of you.' I prised the lid open and stared with some dismay at the gaudy, shocking pink interior. I gulped and pinned as bright a smile as I could to my face.

'But there's over half a tin in here. Surely you could use it yourself?'

'No. Thass alright, my dear. You use it and welcome. I'm glad to help.'

So I thanked her and, clutching the oversized tin in my arms with my shopping, made for the door. As I reached for the handle with some difficulty, it turned suddenly and the door was pulled briskly open, with the result that I lost my balance and literally fell through the opening. My arms opened wide and the paint tin flew up in the air, losing its lid and splashing its contents with abandon over the figure that loomed in front of me. He slipped and fell backwards and, like the paint tin, I followed. When I got my breath back I found I was lying full length on top of a very masculine body.

I gazed down, horrified, into an extremely astonished face, for what seemed like an eternity but could only have been seconds. As I scrambled awkwardly to my feet babbling apologies, that handsome face, liberally splattered with virulent pink, darkened with annoyance.

'What the Hell . . . ' he began and struggled to his own feet, vainly trying to brush off not only the paint but also the washing powder which had burst out of its box and was generously adding to the general mayhem . . .

I prayed for the floor to open and swallow me up but my prayer was unanswered. My path had crossed that of Andrew Bruce's with a vengeance.

Perhaps if I had been more apologetic we could have seen the funny side of it but I rushed in to the attack.

'What a stupid thing to do, yanking the door open like that when I was only just the other side of it and with my arms full.'

I stood leaning forward slightly with my hands on my hips and I'm sure my chin was up. Not exactly conciliatory.

He looked up and glared at me.

'You crazy woman. Just look at me.'

He did indeed look a mess. His hair was coated with blue washing powder and that dreadful pink paint was slowly trickling down from his shoulders and dripping from the bottom of his jacket. Suddenly all I could think of was that I wouldn't have to use it now, after all and I felt an irresistible urge to giggle. I put my hand to my face but he must have seen my expression for his face grew even angrier . . . and then he stilled and stared at me. His gaze slowly raked me from head to toe and I felt my face grow warm, knowing what a disreputable sight I must be.

'Oh, it's you.' His voice was curt. 'I might have known.'

All my amusement fled in an instant. I looked back in desperation at Mrs. Colley who, by this time, had bustled out from behind her counter and was exclaiming at the mess.

She rose nobly to the occasion.

'Don't you worry none, my woman. I'll get my Will to clear that up. It's a good thing none of it got into the shop. Take your jacket off, Mr. Bruce and I'll see what I can do with it.'

He edged past me carefully.

'There's nothing anyone can do with that I'm afraid but if I can just get this stuff off my face that will do for now.' He glared at me once more.

I suppose he was daring me to laugh again but I didn't realise that then. I couldn't bear it.

'Send it to be cleaned,' I said chokingly, 'and send the bill to me.' And, like a coward, took to my heels and fled.

Later on, when I was sure that he was nowhere about, I went back to apologise to Mrs. Colley but she waved my words aside.

'It wasn't as bad as it looked, you know,' she consoled. 'Most of the mess had gone on the gravel and Will got it up with a shovel. Mr. Bruce had a chuckle about it afterwards.'

That I found hard to believe and I felt even more determined to keep out of his way in future.

'Pity about the paint though,' she added. 'It were a real lovely colour.'

4

It was late the next evening when I was just about to go up to bed, that Mrs. Parfitt came in from the kitchen and beckoned to me.

'You know we was talking about young creatures last night,' she said, 'Well, you just come and take a look at this. Not a word to young Jenny, mind. Not yet, that is. Time enough for her to see them in a day or two.'

She pushed at a half open cupboard door under the stairs, opening it wider still and stood aside for me to peer in, a beaming smile on her face. In a cardboard box, lined with an old jumper, was her tabby cat curled snugly round a gently heaving bundle of little furry bodies.

I crouched down and gave the little mother an admiring pat.

'My word, Mrs. Parfitt, you've kept this a secret. When did it happen?'

'Oh, about four weeks ago. Found them there one morning. Mind you, I'd guessed my Sophie was about due. She'd been agitating around that there cupboard for a couple of days. I he'nt said anything about them a 'fore as I didn't want her disturbed.'

She reached down and brought out a protesting small bundle of tabby fur and held the small creature out to me and I took it and held it close.

'Pretty little things, e'nt they? Their eyes are opening now. Your Jenny wouldn't like one, I suppose?'

'Oh, Mrs. Parfitt! You know she'd be over the moon.'

The kitten mewed plaintively, showing a great deal of pink mouth and I laughed and carefully returned it to its mother, who promptly made a great show of washing it from nose to tail.

'Well, if you'd like Jenny to have one she can choose which one she wants in a day or two.'

I thanked her and couldn't help chuckling.

'I guess it's all happening now. I shall have a houseful before I know where I am. I can't wait to get into that little house and have my friend, Peggy, come to visit us,' adding hastily, 'although we've been so very comfortable with you, Mrs. Parfitt.'

She beamed at me and nodded.

'I've enjoyed having the both of you here but I know how it is. There's nothing like having your own place. Well, it won't be long now . . . and, by the way, me name's Dora. Sounds more friendly like if you call me Dora.'

'Only if you call me Emma.' And we smiled at each other in complete accord.

Two days later, I surveyed my small domain with what I like to think of as justifiable pride. Everywhere was clean and bright and the fresh smell of new paint was gradually giving way to the more fragrant one of my favourite lemon-scented furniture polish. The new cooker had been installed the day before and I was now waiting for the carpets and the rest of my furniture to be delivered. I peered into my purse to make sure I had a tip for the delivery men and thought, with some anxiety, of my fast diminishing bank balance. I bit my bottom lip worriedly, hoping I would be able to manage until my first pay cheque arrived. I knew I couldn't expect that until the end of April and then it would only be a small one. I wouldn't get a full month's pay until the end of May. Sighing to myself, I thought of how everything had been more expensive than I had anticipated.

A couple of loud toots from the road outside, heralding the arrival of the furniture van, soon dispelled my uneasy thoughts and the rest of the day was a flurry of activity. By the end of the day all was in place and I had also unpacked the rest of my ubiquitous cardboard boxes. The little house glowed with warmth and comfort . . . a safe haven for myself and Jenny . . . and I promised myself that we would move in the next day. I thought, with pleasure, of Peggy's forthcoming visit and what fun it would be to show her around.

There had been times when I had despaired of ever getting the work done in time for there had been more than one interruption, although I must admit they had been enjoyable ones. Mr. Rawdon had taken me into the school a couple of times to introduce me to everyone and I was very pleased about this for it meant that I wouldn't feel a complete stranger when my first day's teaching finally came around. The other staff members had been welcoming and seemed very pleasant. Young Betty Chapman, whose place I was taking, was leaving at the end of the Spring term to get married and it was quite obvious that her mind was full of wedding plans and little else. She was going to live in Suffolk with her new husband after the wedding.

'Just a little too far for commuting,' she said, with an infectious chuckle.

The other teacher, Catherine Minton,

who took the Reception class, was altogether different. A sober young woman with an earnest air about her, she gave the impression that she took life rather seriously. But she was clearly prepared to be friendly and I felt sure that my Jenny would be in good hands when she started school.

I hadn't realised that there was a big kitchen behind Mr. Rawdon's room and I was very impressed with its immaculate counters and equipment. The young woman who ran it with such efficiency was introduced as Sarah Carter and I shook her hand with pleasure, mainly, I'm ashamed to say, because of thankful thoughts about school dinners. She was an attractive person with merry eyes and a warm smile and in the days to come we became good friends.

There was a happy atmosphere throughout the school and I was reminded irresistibly of my own early schooldays in a very similar small red-brick building. I remarked on this to Mr. Rawdon and he nodded.

'I think most village schools still have this kind of quality, even today. We have as up-to-date equipment as the bigger schools and in no way are we behind them in educational expertise, but we have more of a family feeling. You've been used to a big and rather impersonal school in Manchester, haven't you, Mrs. Dane? I can assure you that you will find us very different.' He smiled down at me and added, 'I can guarantee that you'll enjoy the experience.'

He invited me to his home for a meal one evening and Dora had urged me to go.

'Don't you fret about young Jenny now,' she had said. 'She'll be as right as nine pence along wi' me. It'll do you good to get out. You know what they say about all work and no play and you've been slaving away in that there house from dawn to dusk.'

I laughed at her exaggeration but, knowing that Jenny would be well taken care of, went happily to enjoy my evening off. It was quite a treat to get out of my jeans and sweatshirt for once and dress up a bit. I decided to wear a pale blue wool dress that had a soft deep cowl neckline and cinched my waist in with a darker blue belt, noting with some satisfaction that I could fasten it a notch further than the last time I had worn it. All this hard work was paying dividends.

Mr. Rawdon came to pick me up and drove me to his home in the nearby village of Hudderstone. This was a smart new bungalow and his wife, Elsie, was waiting in the doorway to greet us. She was a bright-eyed, slightly buxom woman who barely reached her husband's shoulder and I took to her instantly.

As we chatted, she told me that she had a part-time job at the local cottage hospital and spoke of it with enthusiasm.

'I'm an SRN and I used to love my nursing when I was a girl. Of course that's a long time ago now. I gave it up when the children came along. Two children we have, Dennis and Jean,' she sighed. 'Both living much too far away.'

Douglas Rawdon regarded his wife with some amusement.

'You'd have them both living at home still, if you could,' he said. 'Tucked under your wings again.'

Turning to me and still grinning, he added, 'Dennis is doing something clever with computers in London and Jean is still at University. Her field is languages.' He gave a small snort of derision. 'Children, indeed!'

But at the same time he put an arm around his wife's shoulders and gave her a hug.

She looked up at him and chuckled.

'Well, I suppose you're right, you aggravating man . . . and they are very good at coming home whenever they can.'

I thought that with such parents those two young people wouldn't need much persuading to come home at every opportunity and must admit to a small feeling of envy . . . which melted away like snow in summer before the Rawdons' combined kindness and hospitality.

The Vicar had knocked on the schoolhouse door one day and, waving away my apologies about the state of my house and my paint-bespattered self, had quite happily seated himself on an upturned packing case and stayed for coffee. He had also brought an invitation for me but this time it was for tea and included Jenny. The Reverend Johnson and his wife lived in a large and rambling vicarage next to the church, which lay at one end of the village and they won Jenny's approval instantly by introducing her to their elderly and affectionate cocker spaniel. The two of them were inseparable all afternoon.

'You'll find we are a friendly community in Little Croxfield, my dear,' the Reverend Johnson said kindly. 'Most of us are on first name terms and you must call us John and Mary. Emma is your name, I believe? Such a nice old-fashioned name.'

He turned to his wife.

'Mary, my dear, you must have a word with Emma about the Mother's Union and the W.I. and all the other activities that go on.'

He picked up his cup and leaned back in his chair, beaming at us both, for all the world like a benevolent cherub.

Before I could think of some tactful response that wouldn't sound completely negative, Mary Johnson raised a quizzical eyebrow and said, 'I rather think we had better let the poor girl get herself settled into her new house and her new job before we start bothering her with any of those things.'

She leaned forward and patted my hand and, with her face hidden from her husband, gave me the merest suspicion of a wink. I felt my lips twitch and hurriedly took a bite of the sandwich in my fingers.

'Perhaps later,' I said. 'It will be

something to look forward to.' And as I spoke, realised with surprise that I actually meant it. I wanted to be involved with what went on in this little Norfolk village. I wanted to belong. So I smiled happily at them both and relaxed and enjoyed the afternoon, feeling sure that I was amongst friends.

Then there had been the day when Jenny and I had been walking down the village street to start on yet another day's activities and had been stopped in our tracks by a loud 'coo-ee' from behind. We turned round to see a large dark-haired young woman, wearing a bright green track suit, jogging along the street towards us, waving frantically. We waited and she caught up with us, breathless and pink-cheeked.

'Thought I'd miss you,' she gasped. 'Tried to catch you the other day but you were off into that little house before I could. I'm Pat Somers. Remember?'

I must have looked as bewildered as I felt for she suddenly grinned, under-standingly.

'Sorry. Of course you won't remember me. I'll bet you were in a daze at the time. I'll remind you. I was at your interview. I'm secretary of our P.T.A. and Douglas press-ganged me into taking part in all the interviews. I might add that I'm jolly glad you got the job.' She held out her hand.

Then I remembered her . . .

'Oh, of course. I knew I'd seen you before,' and, as we shook hands, added, 'To tell you the truth, that interview is still just a blur in my memory. I was petrified at the time.'

'I'm not at all surprised. I remember the last time I had to go for an interview. I was scared witless.'

We laughed and I felt an instant rapport with her.

'I'm off for my morning jog. Come and have coffee with me when I get back?'

'How about you coming to have coffee with me instead? You'll be coming back this way, won't you?' I answered swiftly and was rewarded with a wide smile that lit up Pat's chubby features.

'Great. You're on. To be honest, I'm dying to see what you've been doing in that house. We're all glad to see it looking cared for again. See you soon then.'

With a wave of her hand she trotted away, her dark curly hair bouncing off her shoulders at every step.

Jenny stared after her.

'What a very big lady, Mummy and isn't her pretty suit wobbly.'

'Er . . . yes . . . I suppose it is,' I agreed, hiding a smile. 'But I don't think you should tell her that when she comes back.'

I knew my daughter.

'I'll just tell her that her suit is pretty, shall I?'

And I agreed solemnly that perhaps that would be best.

Later when Pat and I were chatting over coffee, we found that we had much in common and plenty to talk about. I gave her a conducted tour and she admired my handiwork gratifyingly.

'I'm absolutely hopeless at decorating,' she admitted cheerfully, 'but luckily my husband, Bob, is a dedicated handyman. If you ever get stuck with anything just give me a shout and I'll send him over. We don't live far away. Just three doors away from Dora Parfitt. Next to the village shop.'

I gave a sigh of pure envy.

'Do you mean that lovely old flint cottage with the perfectly beautiful front garden?'

'That's right.' Pat looked pleased. 'It is looking rather good just now with all the early spring flowers. I'm the first to admit that I'm useless in the house . . . but I'm in my element in the garden.'

'I shall be coming round for tips,' I assured her.

The only note of discord occurred when the conversation veered round once again to the day of my interview.

'Of course,' Pat declared, 'I told Douglas that we needed someone young for the middle class and that someone with family would be more understanding of childrens' needs. I must say . . . ' and she smiled down at Jenny who, at that moment, was leaning against her knee, absorbed in tracing the pattern on her jog suit with a chubby finger, ' . . . having met your little girl, I'm sure I was right. She's a credit to you.'

Then, obviously without thinking, she added, 'And all except one agreed with me and he . . . ' She stopped short and her hand flew to her mouth. 'Oh, Emma, I'm sorry. I'm so sorry. I shouldn't be talking about that to you at all.'

'Why, you'll be drummed out of the PTA,' I said lightly. 'Don't give it another thought. I shan't.' And the subject was dropped.

But of course, I did, later on. I didn't wonder for long who the dissenter had been. I was quite sure of his identity and gritted my teeth at the thought of his churlishness.

Pat often dropped in after that and friendship grew between us. She had twin boys, two years older than Jenny and they were both in Betty Chapman's class so I would be teaching them after Easter.

'Don't let them give you any nonsense,' warned their mother. 'They can be little devils when they want to be.'

'I've known a few little devils in my time,' I answered blithely. 'If they're anything like their mother we shall get along just fine.'

'Hoo! Flattery will get you everywhere,' she retorted and we grinned at each other.

But, at last, in spite of all the distractions and interruptions, however welcome, our home was ready for Jenny and me and we packed our bags and moved in. Dora had promised to be our first official visitor and was coming to tea the next day.

'For I shall sorely miss the two of you,' she said. 'It's been lovely to have someone to cook and do for again.'

That first evening in my little house, after Jenny had been tucked up in her 'garden room' as she insisted on calling it, along with her favourite and tatty old bear, I wandered about happily, running my hand over the satin-smooth wood of the pine dresser, adjusting a picture here and tweaking a curtain into a more becoming fold there. The open fire flickered and glowed in the hearth of the old Norfolk brick fireplace, its reflection gleaming in the well-polished brass fire irons that had once belonged to my Aunt Maggie and which I had now returned to their right and proper place on a country hearth. I sank into the comfy fireside chair with a sigh of contentment and, kicking off my shoes, stretched out my toes to the warmth of the fire. I'll ring Pegs tomorrow, I thought dreamily, and tell her we've moved in at last.

For no reason at all and quite unbidden, except that I was probably so relaxed that all my defences were down,

Pat's words, 'And all except one agreed with me,' crept insidiously into my mind and my stomach muscles tightened and my fists clenched and my peace of mind fled.

Why? I wondered, yet again. Why was that wretched man so against me? What had I ever done to him? It was as if he had a personal grudge against me. Even if I did remind him of his fickle girlfriend I can't help my looks. Then I remembered that awful pink paint and thought ruefully that perhaps he would have a grudge against me now after that episode in the shop doorway.

A feeling of desolation swept over me out of all proportion and I thumped my fist angrily on the chair arm. 'I can do without this,' I said out loud and my thoughts ran on. No way was I ever going to let any man make me feel like this again. He was nothing to me and I certainly didn't need . . . or want . . . his approval. I shrugged angrily and reached across to turn my radio on. The strains of Schubert's music softly filled the room and I leaned back against the cushions and gave myself a mental shake.

You're getting paranoid, my girl, I told myself. Most of this is probably just your imagination. I expect he merely thought that one of the other candidates would fit in better than you, that's all and he's perfectly entitled to do that. So to hell with him. You got the job anyway. With that, I resolutely banished all thoughts of dissension . . . and keen blue eyes and dark untidy hair . . . to those hidden recesses of my mind.

The Easter holidays arrived and all was quiet in the school buildings next door. Peggy was due to arrive and both Jenny and I were looking forward with great anticipation to her visit.

'She's here, Mummy! She's here!' Jenny rushed into the house through the open front door and then wheeled around and rushed out again and down the garden path. I followed almost as quickly. Peggy was getting rather stiffly

111

out of her car and was greeted with a whirlwind of hugs from us both. Grabbing her hand, Jenny did her best to drag her through the gate.

'Oh, come on, Auntie Pegs. I've got such a lot to show you. Just you wait until you see what I've got.'

'Whoa there. Hold on, girl. That's just what I intend to do . . . wait. You hang on a tick until I've got my things out of the car.'

All of us laden, we walked up the path, laughing and chattering happily.

'Look, Auntie Pegs. Isn't she beautiful?'

Jenny had run ahead and now came back to meet us, carefully carrying a small sleepy bundle of tabby fur. Two round blue eyes blinked owlishly as Peggy gently stroked the kitten's velvety head.

'When did you aquire her?' she asked me.

'Only yesterday and Jenny can't bear to be away from her for a minute. She wanted to take her to bed with her last night.'

'Of course. What else did you expect?'

'There. You see, Mummy. Auntie Pegs thinks it's alright.'

Peggy looked at me and laughed.

'That wasn't exactly what I meant, love. You'll be getting me into dead trouble with your Mum.'

I ushered Peggy through the front door and we dumped her belongings in the hallway.

'Oh, Pegs. It is good to see you.'

'Me too. God. I've missed you both.' Peggy's voice was suddenly gruff and we both looked at each other and blew our noses and sniffed and laughed.

'Well, come on, give me a guided tour round the estate then and let's see what you've been doing with yourself all this time.'

'Cup of tea first. You must be ready for one after that long journey. You managed to find us alright?'

She followed me into the kitchen.

'Oh, yes. No problem at all. I say, Em, you wouldn't by any remote chance have made a coffee cake to go with that cuppa, would you? You've no idea how I've missed your cooking.'

I reached down a large tin from a shelf and handed it to her with a chuckle.

'There you go, pal. As if I'd forget.'

I'd well remembered Peggy's passion for my gooey coffee cake and it had been first on my list of jobs that morning.

After our tea the school house was inspected and admired and then we walked round the outside of the school next door, peering in the windows.

'Douglas . . . Mr. Rawdon, that's the Head, remember? . . . said that I can borrow the key from the caretaker during the holidays if I want, so I can show you round properly later on. It's very different from Norton.'

'I'll say. Isn't it tiny! How many will you have in your class? Twenty-two wasn't it? What bliss. I've got thirty-eight this year.'

As we strolled back to the house,

Peggy looked around her and then said, 'I tell you what, Em, as I'm here for a week and have got the car, how about if I take you and Jenny exploring the countryside? I've never been in Norfolk before and I'm willing to bet that you haven't been outside those four walls since you came down here.'

'You'd lose your bet then,' I said airily. 'I've been simply inundated with invitations.' And, laughing at her disbelieving look, I took her arm and steered her back indoors.

'Well, you're almost right. I must admit that would be nice and Jenny would love it.' I smiled down at her and ruffled her curls. 'She's been so good while I've been up to my eyes in things.'

'That's settled then. We'll make plans this evening.'

Over our evening meal, Peggy turned to Jenny. 'Where shall we go first, poppet? You can choose our first trip.'

'Everywhere.' She clapped her hands and bounced up and down, clearly delighted at the thought of the treats ahead and then got down from her chair and ran to me.

'Mummy, where can we go?'

I lifted her on my knee and hugged her.

'I'll tell you all sorts of places and then you can choose. You deserve some treats because you really have been good while I've been so busy. Auntie Pegs can choose next and then it will be my turn.'

So the holiday week was spent in exploring the Norfolk that I remembered so well and that Peggy and my little daughter had never seen. We walked along the sandy beaches at Wells-Next-the-Sea and back through the sand dunes and into the pine woods that flanked them and Jenny raced up and down the hills and hollows and scrambled on the the low branches of ancient twisted pines as countless children had done before, myself included. Trees that were worn to a polished smoothness by generations of such clambering.

We trudged through the shingly beaches at Cley, admiring the great windmill that stands looking out to sea and had great difficulty in restraining Jenny from filling the car boot with a multitude of smooth and pretty pebbles. We investigated other windmills and went for a boat ride on the Broads and were all delighted to spy an old grey heron sleepily standing on one leg among the reeds.

We picnicked in Sandringham woods and followed one of the nature trails in spite of chill east winds and could hardly drag Jenny away from the delights of a close-by wild life park. That had been a new one for me as well as it had only been open a few years and they could hardly drag me away either. Peggy was equally enthusiastic about the stately homes of Blickling and Holkham.

One day Peggy and I had just for ourselves and while Jenny spent the day quite happily with Dora, we went to Norwich and trawled the shops and went to the theatre. Peggy had to admit that the shops, theatre, cinemas and library were as good as any in Manchester, if not better.

'It's a splendid city,' she agreed. 'But you know, Em, you'll have to get yourself a car. You really need your own transport here.'

I couldn't have agreed with her more, but pointed out that I would have to wait for a long time before I could afford such a luxury.

By the end of her stay Peggy acknowledged that she was much happier about my venture.

'I shall still miss you but I shan't worry about you now. You've got a nice cosy little home here, a good job and, by all accounts, a decent headmaster and really, I have to say that Norfolk is a lovely area to live in. But you will keep in touch regularly, won't you?'

I put my arms round her and hugged her.

'Of course I will. You're family and don't you forget it.'

'Right,' she said, briskly and turned to Jenny, but I glimpsed a suspicion of brightness in her eyes before she turned away.

'Now then, chick. I've one day left. What would you like to do, most of all?'

There was no hesitation at all.

'Oh, Auntie Pegs, could we go and get my puppy? Mummy said we had to wait until you came and ... and ... I've waited and waited ... and ... and ... Oh, could we, please?'

Peggy looked across at me with raised eyebrows and an almost comical look of dismay.

'Well,' I said slowly, 'I did promise her, Pegs. I suppose we could go and see this Mr. Bruce. Dora said he would be the one to ask about any pups to be had around here.'

I shrugged away my unwillingness and made up my mind.

'Alright, love. We'll walk down to see him in a little while. Mind you,' I said, warningly, 'Don't expect to get a puppy today. But we will go and see what we can find out. O.K., Pegs?'

'If you say so. Who's this Mr. Bruce?'

'The local vet. Don't you remember. I'm sure I told you. He's one of the school governors and was at my interview.'

'Mm, yes. I remember,' she grinned at me provokingly. 'The tall, stern and handsome one. Wasn't there something about blue eyes?'

She looked at me, blandly.

'Oh, shut up, Pegs. I wish I'd never mentioned that.'

'You threw a tin of paint over him as well, didn't you?'

'Oh, don't. That was awful. I could have sunk through the floor. I did write him a note to apologise and offered to pay his cleaning bill and got a curt little note in return, telling me not to give it another thought. I just hope that's the end of it.'

'Well, we shall soon find out. Come on, let's go and meet this charmer.'

'Oh, hush, Pegs . . . little pigs, and all that . . . ' I pushed my hair off my face and spoke a shade crossly. 'He's a long way from being that anyway.'

Jenny had been looking up at us, interestedly.

'Where are they?' she asked.

'Where are what, love?'

'The little pigs.'

That rather restored my good humour and I made some non-committal answer, giggling as I caught Peggy's eye.

'We haven't far to go,' I said, as I zipped up Jenny's jacket. 'Dora told me his house is at the far end of the village. The big one with the twisted chimneys.'

Peggy, who had been taken to meet Dora at the beginning of her stay, remarked as I closed the door behind us.

'Isn't she a nice little woman, your Mrs. Parfitt.'

'Yes, she is. I wish you could have met the Rawdons and Pat Somers but they won't be back from their holidays until after you have gone home.'

'Never mind. Next time. Pat sounds nice from what you've told me. I'm glad there's someone around that's our age.'

We walked up the village street, answering the various cheerful greetings from people working in their gardens and Peggy remarked that everyone seemed very friendly and I agreed with her. In fact I felt as if I belonged already. Jenny skipped along in front of us and reached the tall wrought iron gates of Croxfield Hall well ahead and stood waiting, staring up the driveway towards the old red-brick house with eager eyes.

Peggy gave a low whistle as we caught up with her.

'I'm impressed. Lord of the Manor is he then, this vet of yours?'

'No, nothing like that.' I held out a hand to an impatient Jenny. 'Apparently his parents bought the place when it was in a very sorry state. Part of it had even begun to fall down. They have spent a lot of time and hard work on it since, doing it up.'

'Well, they've made a splendid job of it.' She gazed round admiringly. 'They must have an army of gardeners though to look after this little patch. Isn't it beautiful?'

'Pat told me that Mrs. Bruce does most of it single handed. She's another green-fingered enthusiast.'

We started to walk down the drive, enjoying the glorious colours of the flowers that lined our way. Early pink tulips jostled with daffodils and clumps of brilliant yellow and purple crocus pushed their way through the taller stems of sweet scented narcissus. Behind these, grape hyacinths had been mass planted to make a river of blue, the colour of a summer sky, that wound its way between shrubs that were also beginning to burst into bloom.

'It's breathtaking,' I agreed. 'She must work awfully hard. It's sad, really. Old Mr. Bruce used to be the local vet but he's gradually becoming crippled with arthritis and is practically confined to a wheelchair now. It's his son we are going to see. His practice was some-where up in Yorkshire. I think he was a junior partner actually but he gave it up to come back here and take over from his father.'

'This Mrs. Bruce?'

'Oh, she's his mother.'

'My, my, you are well informed!' Peggy's voice was dry and she gave me a knowing look.

'It's just Dora's gossiping. I could hardly get away from it when I was staying there. You'd be surprised how much I know about everyone in the village already.'

But I felt my face grow warm.

By this time we had reached the side door and entrance to a small waiting room. I looked at my watch.

'We've timed that well. It should be the end of surgery time according to our Dora. I didn't want to take up his time with this business of a puppy if there was anyone waiting with a sick animal.'

Jenny tugged at my restraining hand and peered into the waiting room.

'There's no-one there, Mummy. Can

I knock on the door?'

'Push that button, love. It will probably ring a bell.'

She reached up to a push button on a shelf by the surgery door but before she could press it, the door opened and Andrew Bruce came out. No doubt alerted by the sound of our voices. He looked across Jenny's head at me and the beginnings of a smile on his face faded completely and his face hardened.

'Yes,' he said, coolly. 'What can I do for you?'

During the few weeks I had been in Little Croxfield I had met nothing but welcome and kindness. Although I had been very conscious of this man's unspoken antagonism at the time of my interview, I really had made an effort to push it to the back of my mind, telling myself that most of it was due to my overactive imagination. That I felt a certain amount of nervousness at the thought of meeting him again was, I felt, due to something entirely different although I couldn't . . . or, perhaps wouldn't . . . understand what. Be that as it may, my defences were down and I was totally unprepared for the rebuff that was manifest in his set face. I was at a loss and my first impulse was to babble some excuse and beat a hasty retreat. It was Jenny's tug at my sleeve that recalled me to the purpose of our visit and I took a deep breath and straightened my shoulders.

'Good morning, Mr. Bruce.' My voice was as cool as his. 'I've been told that you would probably know if there are any puppies for sale in the district. Crossbred, preferably. I would be most grateful if you could give me any information.'

I felt, rather than saw, Peggy give a sideways look at me and Jenny's fingers crept into my hand.

Andrew Bruce folded his arms across his chest and looked down at me.

'Excuse me for saying this, er . . . Mrs. Dane, isn't it?'

For some reason my throat felt dry and I swallowed and raised my chin a fraction higher. There was more than a tinge of disapproval in his voice.

'But how exactly do you propose to bring up a pup in your circumstances?'

I stared at him unbelievingly and felt my face grow warm.

'I'm afraid I don't understand you. I can assure you that I am perfectly capable of looking after a puppy.'

'I don't doubt that.' His voice was sarcastic. 'Given the time and opportunity and always providing that it didn't give you more responsibility than you could handle. But what about when you are at school and the poor little begger is left on its own? Or are you proposing to nip across to see it every half hour or so? Just because you were given the house next to the school you mustn't think you have the freedom to do that, you know.'

The warmth left my face and I felt an icy anger. I couldn't believe my ears. I glared at him furiously.

'I can assure you, Mr. Bruce, that I have absolutely no intention of taking advantage of the fact that I live next to the school and I am quite aware of my responsibilities. I certainly do not need you to point them out to me.'

I poured all the contempt and scorn that I felt towards his churlish behaviour into my next words.

'I don't think we will waste any more of your valuable time. Good morning.'

Just before I whirled around, I caught a glimpse of a strange expression flitting across his face. It might almost have been one of horror but I didn't stay to question it. Seizing Jenny's hand and grabbing Peggy by the arm, I marched them both off down the drive as fast as I decently could.

Jenny's plaintive little voice drifted up to me.

'Don't we get a puppy then, Mummy?'

But I couldn't speak.

'Phew!' said Peggy as we turned into the village street. 'Slow down, girl, slow down. What on earth was that all about? I thought the two of you were going to come to blows. What an objectionable man. I take back all I had been thinking about him.'

'Oh, Pegs,' I answered dolefully. 'I just seem to have got on the wrong side of him altogether. To tell you the truth, he has got a point.'

'What rubbish. As if . . . '

'I mean about the puppy being on its own,' I interrupted her. 'I was a bit impulsive when I promised Jenny a puppy and I have been wondering if it was sensible with me being out for most of the day.'

I looked down at my little daughter and gently ruffled her hair. 'But you know I always like to keep my word to her.'

Jenny looked up with a sparkle of tears in her eyes.

'You promised, Mummy,' she said reproachfully.

'Let's go home and talk about it,' suggested Peggy. 'I think we've got just a little bit of a problem.' She squeezed my arm. 'Don't look so worried, Em. We'll sort something out.'

Back at the house and settled down

with comforting cups of coffee, Peggy asked quietly, 'Now, Em. What exactly is bothering you? Is it the thought of leaving a puppy on its own, is it about not keeping your word to Jenny or is it about getting on the wrong side of that young man?'

I gave an indignant snort, glad that Jenny had taken her kitten out into the garden.

'Huh! It's certainly nothing to do with Mr. High and Mighty Bruce. Insufferable man. I hope I never have to set eyes on him again.'

'Hmm. Well that takes care of that question. Now, what about the others?'

In the end we decided that perhaps a puppy wasn't such a good idea after all. At least, not yet. Calling Jenny in from the garden, we put it to her. Surprisingly, she was very amenable about it.

'After all, Mummy, I have got my Tabitha and she does take a lot of looking after. P'raps I wouldn't have time to look after a puppy as well.'

Hoisting the kitten further up in her

arms, she ran out into the garden again.

'Kids!' I meant to speak lovingly but must admit to a touch of exasperation. 'Here have I been worrying. You know, Pegs, perhaps I will be the one to mind not having a dog, rather than Jenny.'

'That wouldn't surprise me at all.' She laughed and poured me another cup of coffee.

All too soon we were waving goodbye to her as she set off back to Manchester and I had to turn my thoughts to the beginning of the Summer term in Croxfield school. During Peggy's stay we had found time to go into the building while the caretaker was busy with the cleaning and we had investigated the classroom which was to be mine and peeped into all the others.

We both agreed that Douglas Rawdon had spoken with truth about the up-to-date equipment, for the books and teaching aids were as good as any we had used in our big Manchester school. The classrooms were bright and cheerful and the children's furniture a delight.

'And look, Pegs,' I had said, 'lots of cupboard space. I'm really going to enjoy teaching here.'

The first day arrived at last. By now, Jenny had made friends with several children in the village so she skipped off quite happily to be made much of by the bigger girls while I crossed the playground and went in to join Douglas and Catherine. When I faced my class of six- and seven-year-olds it was as if I had never been away from teaching for those five and a half years and the day flashed by as we spent time getting to know one another and sorting out books and pencils and the hundred and one other things necessary for the smooth running of an Infant's class.

There was the inevitable, naughty small boy who tried his tricks on me but I wasn't without experience and, besides, I had always had rather a soft spot for such imps and soon managed to direct his energies to more profitable pastimes. I felt sure we were all going to get along splendidly and hoped, by the end of the day, that the children would feel the same. Douglas popped his head in during the afternoon, but seeing them all clustered around my chair as I read them a story, apart from the youngest one who was practically asleep, snuggled on my knee, merely grinned and nodded his head in, what I hoped was a satisfied sort of way, before slipping back into his own room.

At the end of the afternoon, when I had seen the last of my children safely off the premises and made the aquaintance of more of the mothers who had come to collect their offspring and was just about to fetch Jenny, Douglas came into my classroom.

'Well, how did it go then, your first day?'

'Splendidly . . . I think. It's been a sort of blur, really.' We both laughed.

'First days are usually like that, aren't they. But out of chaos comes order . . . hopefully. Now, there is something that I meant to tell you before this but every time I thought about it something else cropped up to distract me. You will have another pupil tomorrow. He is a little different from the rest of your children and tends to get over excited. Which is why we encourage his mother to bring him in on the second day of term rather than the first. He's a Down's Syndrome child.'

He looked at me enigmatically and then added, 'You will find that the other children accept him well. In fact most of them are quite protective of him.'

I don't know what he expected to see in my face. As it happened, there had been a similar child in my last class at Norton Primary. A most loving little girl and one that I had loved in return. I gave him what I hoped was a reassuring smile and told him that I'd had experience with such children and he nodded.

'Yes, I did know that. Your previous headmistress wrote and told me when I got in touch with her.'

I wondered what had been said and Douglas looked at me and laughed.

'Don't look so worried. The letter was all to your credit. Now, off you go and get that cup of tea that I'm sure you're longing for.'

The burly, grey haired man smiled down at me and patted me on the shoulder and I grinned back, thankfully.

Jenny's glowing face peeped round the doorway then. 'Mummy, are you ready yet? Miss Minton said I could come and find you.'

'Yes, sweetheart, I'm ready. Let's go home.'

As I spoke, I felt a deep and sure satisfaction. I felt at home in this little village, in the rosy-red brick school, in my school house and, most of all, with the people around me. Catching hold of Jenny's hand, I whisked her, laughing, across the playground. Everything's lovely I thought . . . except . . . except . . . but before my wayward thoughts could even take shape I banished them and concentrated instead on Jenny's excited account of her first day at school.

The first two weeks of the term sped

by quickly and by then I was settled in and passably well organised in the classroom and any spare time I had managed to find had been used to finish off jobs around the house. The following weekend we were blessed with such beautiful spring weather that I knew I just had to get out into the wilderness which passed for a garden and begin to restore it to some kind of law and order.

It would not be true to say this was my first garden for the house I had lived in with Jimmy had a miniscule open plan front garden and quite a large patch of lawn at the back surrounded by shrubs. But it had all been planted out before we moved in and all I had to do was keep it tidy. This garden was something else. I would quite definitely have to start from scratch and whatever finished result I achieved would be my very own.

Once the breakfast dishes were cleared away I fetched Aunt Maggie's gardening books from my bookcase.

She had left me quite a selection and now could be the time to put them to good use. I could have spent all that Saturday morning poring over them and making plans but saw the sense of leaving that until later. Now was the time for a bit of spade work. Literally.

Wearing an oldish pair of jeans and a sweater and with my hair tied up in a pony tail I began the Herculean task of digging up the nettles which seemed to have crept into every space. Jenny, wanting to help, bravely tried to pile the rubbish up but gave up rather quickly, complaining that the plants bit her.

'Well, they are called stinging nettles and I did warn you, poppet.' I commiserated. 'Come here and let me rub your hand with this big dock leaf. That will make it better.'

I smiled to myself, remembering Aunt Maggie telling me exactly the same. She was a bit dubious but the charm worked and she skipped off to take some dandelion leaves to the white rabbits.

The ground was soft and the weeds came up with surprising ease and, as I progressed, I began to see outlines of what had once been flower beds and realised that perhaps my task would not be as difficult as I had first thought. Daffodils and tulips were struggling through the weeds and the more I searched the more signs I found of what surely had to be some kinds of flowering plants. I shall have to ask Elsie Rawdon, I thought. After all it was once her garden. Perhaps she can tell me what to look out for. She had told me that she used to keep it in reasonable order and had been quite sad to see it so neglected.

It was while I was on my knees, carefully teasing out tufts of grass from a large clump of purple and yellow crocus, that I heard the garden gate give its customary groan. I really must give that gate some oil, I thought, and pushed myself to my feet, dusting my hands on the seat of my jeans.

I turned round, half expecting to see

Pat coming along the path as she had promised to come and give me a hand some time during the day.

Instead, to my surprise and consternation, I saw Andrew Bruce advancing towards me.

5

Andrew Bruce walked slowly towards me and for a split second I considered flight. Then bravado kicked in and I jabbed my garden fork into the ground with all the force I could muster, straightened up, put my hands on my hips and glared at him. It was weird how that man seemed to bring out hostility in me. I wasn't usually so aggressive.

He stopped short and I could have sworn that the corners of his mouth twitched. Holding up his hands in mock surrender, he said solemnly,

'Don't shoot. I'm unarmed.'

Don't think I wouldn't . . . if I only had a gun . . . I thought, resentfully, for that telltale twitch, seemingly so out of character, had thrown me into confusion. Tearing my gaze away from his mouth, I stared at him doubtfully.

'I've come to apologise,' he said.

He took a step nearer and a tentative smile lit his face.

'I have no doubt at all that I deserve your fury. What I said to you the other day was unforgivable I know. I . . . I don't know what came over me. I really am sorry.'

In the face of such an apology, what could I do? But still my tongue wouldn't work and like a fool, I just blinked and couldn't find the words.

He lowered his hands and his diffident smile began to falter and I suppose it was his hesitancy that banished mine and I found my voice at last. I looked away from him and took a deep steadying breath.

'Well, you did have a point . . . about the puppy.' I wasn't going to forgive him so easily for his other accusation. 'If I'm honest, I was doubtful about that. In a thoughtless moment I made a promise to my little girl and I happen to believe that promises should be kept, if at all possible . . . especially to children.'

I looked at him then and saw unmistakable relief in his eyes. I made up my mind and said briskly,

'You were quite right, Mr. Bruce. I wouldn't have been able to look after a puppy satisfactorily. Anyway, I've decided to shelve the idea for the time being, although,' and I suppose I must have sounded wistful, 'it would have been lovely to have a dog around,'

The colour crept up his face.

'Please forget my boorish behaviour of the other day. Was your little girl very disappointed?'

I felt the beginnings of a smile.

'Well, no, she wasn't really. She has a kitten you see and all her attention seems to be taken up with that.'

His face cleared. 'But would you still like a dog? How about an older one?'

'Oh, yes. But that wouldn't be so easy. Where would I look?'

Jenny, who had been playing with Tabitha in the long grass, came up to us then and, pressing up against me, looked up at Andrew Bruce with big solemn eyes. He hunkered down level with her and said gently, 'Would you do me a big favour?'

She turned and looked up at me and I smiled down at her and shrugged my shoulders, mystified.

He stood up agilely and turned to go back down the path, beckoning to us both to follow and leading us to his slightly shabby estate car which was parked on the grass verge.

A black and white border collie pushed a moist enquiring muzzle through the slightly open window and I gazed into melting, pansy brown eyes . . . and was lost.

'Now, about this favour,' he said, looking down at Jenny. 'If your Mummy agrees, do you think you could look after Jess, here? You see, she has lost her master and has nowhere to live.'

Jenny looked up at me eagerly but I'm sure she saw, by the look on my face, that she had no need to ask.

'You really will be doing me a favour.' he continued, turning to me. 'The old

143

chap that Jess belonged to died recently and none of his family can take her. They've asked me to find a home for her and I thought she'd probably be ideal for you. She's five years old, well trained and healthy. She's also been spayed so you won't have any problems on that score and she'll cope with being left on her own for a few hours at a time. What do you think?'

I could hardly believe my ears but felt a huge smile spreading over my face.

'What do I think? Oh, Mr. Bruce, it would be wonderful. I don't know how to thank you.'

'Andrew, please . . . and I must thank you.'

He ran his fingers through his unruly hair and said rather more stiffly,

'We got off to a bad start, didn't we? Let's just say . . . er . . . no more paint jobs, eh?'

I felt my face grow warm then but we both laughed and he turned and opened the car door and the dog jumped down to sniff cautiously at my offered hand. Jenny had no such inhibitions but flung her arms round Jess's neck before either of us could restrain her. There was no need to worry for it was obviously love at first sight for both of them.

I looked back at Andrew, still laughing only to find that he was staring at me in the oddest way with a kind of arrested look on his face. Then he shook his head and spoke briskly, handing me Jess's lead.

'Right. Here you are then. I'll be off. Any problems, just let me know.'

He raised his hand and quickly got into his car and drove off as if the devil was at his heels.

I felt confused as I watched him go. What had happened to change him so? Although perhaps he wasn't all that changed. His manner was still curt. Anyway, I told myself, at least he must have realised that he was wrong about me and that I wasn't as irresponsible as he had seemed to think. He had made amends with giving me Jess so now honours were even and I needn't think about him any more. Catching myself up on that thought, I told myself that I really hadn't been thinking about him anyway. So why did my heart feel so much lighter?

To clear my head of my muddled thoughts I looked down at Jenny who was sitting on the ground at my feet, stroking Jess's soft coat and crooning to her.

'Jenny, love, I think we had better take Jess up to the house and let her meet Tabitha there. We must be careful because she may not be used to kittens.'

That evening, long after Jenny had been tucked up in bed, I sat by the dying fire with Jess's head resting on my knee. I stroked the silky fur absently, conjuring up a memory of broad shoulders and rugged features that were no longer harsh and uncompromising but held a hint of a smile. When I started to visualise those vivid blue eyes looking down into mine I suddenly realised what I was doing and came to my senses with a start. I jumped to my feet and hurried into the kitchen to make a hot drink.

'Bedtime, Jess,' I said firmly. 'Come along, girl. This blanket will do for now. No more nonsense.'

She thumped her feathery tail, dislodging the kitten who had been patting it with playful paws and followed me in. She looked up at me then as if to say that she wasn't the one who had been guilty of nonsense.

The days flew past and I settled back into teaching as if I had never been away and managed to assimilate the newer ideas and methods fairly easily. I found Douglas Rawdon to be a tower of strength and easy to work with. He was a man of such boundless enthusiasm that the children in his care responded with eagerness and enjoyment. Catherine who took the Reception class was a very quiet young woman with a rather serious outlook but was an able, sympathetic teacher and my Jenny was very happy with her. It soon became obvious that she had disapproved of my predecessor, thinking her flighty and unreliable. I must admit that I found evidence that Betty's teaching had not been as sound as it should have been but I remembered how the children had clustered round her, happy and secure and I found excuses for her, thinking that the girl had probably had her head full of wedding plans for the last few months anyway.

We all worked together very well and when I wrote to Peggy I told her what a happy place the village school was.

'I feel as if I belong here already,' I wrote. 'We're like one big family. That's one of the advantages of a village school. Norton could be a bit impersonal and as for that big Middle school nearby, if you remember the headmaster admitted that he didn't even know all his staff particularly well, let alone the children. I wish you could see my class. I've only got twenty two. Heaven after the big classes I was used to. I feel that I will be able to give each child so much more time. They are a mixed bunch but then, what class isn't? Some are bright and some never will be.'

'I've got one Holy Terror! Remember your Jacko, last year? This one is three times as bad. His name is George and rumour has it that his dad is the local poacher. Wherever there is mischief in the village that boy is in the thick of it. He caused mayhem with the local football team last week by dashing on to the field in the middle of a match and making off with the ball. They were not very pleased at having to retrieve it from a large patch of nettles! I have to watch him like a hawk in the classroom but he's got such a cheeky grin that I can't help having a soft spot for him.

'On the whole they are super kids and their parents are so supportive. Perhaps they don't have all the material benefits that town children have and several of the families are quite poor, I suppose, in comparison. Farm workers don't get terribly well paid. Yet I feel they are rich in other ways. They are much healthier for one thing and it shows in their clear skins and rosy cheeks . . . '

Although I enthused about my work in my letters to Peggy and had a great deal to tell her of life in the village and of how Jenny had taken to it all like a little duck to water and also of my growing friendship with Pat Somers, for some reason I didn't want to talk of Andrew Bruce. I merely mentioned that we had settled our differences and that perhaps our first encounters had been misleading and told her about Jess.

However, I did tell her that I had made friends with Gwen Bruce.

Shortly after I had aquired Jess, there had been a knock at my door one early evening and I opened it to a sweet-faced woman with greying hair, wearing serviceable navy cord trousers and a matching jacket. She smiled and held out her hand.

'Hello, my dear. I'm Gwen Bruce. I live at the end of the village and thought it was time that I called to make myself known and wish you well.'

I clasped her hand readily.

'Why, how nice of you. Do come in.'

'Well, just for a minute then. I'm sure you want to relax after a hard day at school and don't really want visitors.'

I smiled and shook my head and asked her to stay for a coffee and we chatted for quite a while. As she got up to go she told me how she admired the way I had been tackling the overgrown garden and when I said, ruefully, that it was a very uphill task, offered to bring me some plants from her garden. Needless to say I accepted that offer with alacrity and a few days later she was as good as her word and turned up with a carrier bag full of all sorts of bits and pieces. Not only that, she stayed to help and advise me and we spent a very enjoyable hour together. Before she left, she asked me if Jenny and I would like to go over the next day for Sunday lunch with her and her husband.

I own I was a bit surprised to get this invitation on such short acquaintance and was also hesitant about socialising with Andrew. Some sixth sense warned me that there could be danger in further contact. A danger that might well be exhilarating but would also threaten the peace of mind and quiet contentment that I was striving for in this new life.

But I should imagine that when Gwen Bruce set herself out to charm, very few people could resist her and I was no exception. Besides, I told myself, there was no need to blame the mother because the son had once been a bit churlish.

'We'd always hoped we'd have a little girl after Andrew,' she confided. 'But it just didn't happen. If you brought Jenny over, my Arthur would be delighted I know. He loves to meet new people and he doesn't get out much with that wretched arthritis plaguing him. You really would be doing him a favour.'

I looked at her a little sharply then, for I had heard differently. Arthur

Bruce apparently got about all over the place in his wheelchair and in his car in spite of his disability. But she met my glance blandly, continuing, 'I doubt that Andrew will be able to join us though. He has quite a few appointments tomorrow.'

If she noticed the shuttered look I had pinned to my face at the mention of her son's name, followed by the relief I felt at the thought of his absence, she made no sign of it.

Jenny and I walked up the village street the next morning, Jenny filled with anticipation but I with mixed feelings. I had felt relief when Gwen had said that Andrew would not be there for lunch and then, later, filled with an illogical disappointment.

In some ways Gwen reminded me of my dear Aunt Maggie and from our first meeting I had felt myself responding to her warmth and kindness. When I met Arthur Bruce I found him to be a man of charm and dry good humour. He struggled to his feet to take my hand in spite of my protests and as I looked up into his keen blue eyes, so like his son's, I realised that here was a man of great strength of character.

Over lunch, which was an enjoyable informal affair, he and I discovered a mutual passion for chess, so afterwards Gwen took Jenny off to inspect the 'zoo', as she called the compound where recuperating and stray animals were kept.

'We will leave you two to indulge in your sport,' she said. 'I can see that the light of battle is in your eyes. You won't mind if we are a long time, will you? I think a donkey ride is more our idea of fun.'

Jenny's eyes lit up and as she eagerly took hold of Gwen's outstretched hand, Arthur grinned and answered.

'Who's going to enjoy that most? No, my dear, be as long as you like. Emma and I have some serious business to attend to.'

I stared and then laughed as he turned to a small table at his side and opened up a chess board.

'You would like a game?' he questioned. 'Please do go with Gwen and Jenny if you would rather.'

'I would love a game,' I said promptly. 'Really I would. My aunt taught me to play when I was quite small. She was a real enthusiast. I've really missed playing.'

We bent over the board and time slid past. When Gwen and Jenny returned, both slightly breathless and muddy, it was to find two people completely in accord with one another.

'My word, Gwen, I enjoyed that.'

'By the look on your face, Arthur, I take it that you won?'

Her husband grinned.

'Yes, as a matter of fact I did. But it wasn't easy. This young woman gave me a hard fight.'

'I'm out of practice,' I said composedly. 'Just you wait until next time.'

'Right! You're on. Soon, I hope.'

Gwen gave me a wide smile.

'I can just about manage a game with

him, Emma, but he beats me every time so it's not much fun for him. You'll enjoy a challenge, won't you, Arthur? Andrew plays well but, of course, he never has much opportunity. There's always a call for him whenever he thinks he has some spare time. Today, for instance, he has been called out urgently. There's a foal about to be born and the mare is having difficulties.'

I leaned back in my chair and Jenny climbed on to my lap.

'Oh, Mummy, I had a ride on old Moke and he is lovely and you should see the animals in the zoo. There's lots and lots and there's a big dog with his leg all wrapped up in bandages, poor thing.'

Jenny was full of her experiences and reluctant to leave. So was I, for that matter . . . but it was time to go. It was while we were saying our goodbyes in the doorway that Andrew drove up. As I saw his car turn in at the gateway my heart seemed to flip over and I caught my breath. Quickly I bent down to Jenny.

'Say goodbye and thank you, darling.'

I straightened up as he came towards us, in control of myself again.

'Good afternoon, Mr. Br . . . er . . . Andrew . . . we're just on our way home. What a shame you missed your lunch.' I kept my voice cool.

He nodded briefly.

'Please excuse me. I need to clean up.'

I could have sworn I heard an exasperated sigh behind me but when I turned towards Gwen she was smiling serenely.

Jenny, however, had no inhibitions. To her, Andrew was the one who had brought her darling Jess and consequently a best friend.

'Hello, Mr. Bruce,' she beamed at him and his face softened as he looked down.

'Why, hello, Jenny. How's Jess?'

'She's fine and ever so good, isn't she, Mummy?'

'Yes, she is. She's obviously been well trained. She's very obedient and we love her to bits.'

Jenny gave a gentle tug at Andrew's jacket.

'Did that baby foal get borned?'

He smiled. 'Yes he did . . . and he's a fine strong little fellow.'

'Why don't you take Jenny to see him?' suggested Gwen. 'I'm sure she'd love that. Come to think of it, so would Emma. I gather she's as horse-mad as you are.'

'Oh, yes please.' Jenny hopped from one foot to another in her excitement.

'Jenny, Mr. Bruce must be far too busy for that,' I said, hoping that I wasn't sounding too ungracious.

She gave me such a doleful look that neither Andrew nor I could help laughing and so arrangements were made and Gwen waved us off with what looked suspiciously like satisfaction. But I felt he had been press-ganged into it all and was uncomfortably doubtful about his sentiments.

He had arranged to take us to see the new foal on the next Saturday and the day dawned, bright and clear. I rifled through my wardrobe indecisively, wondering what to wear. Pulling out a pretty full-skirted yellow dress of fine cotton, I held it up against myself and turned to look in the long mirror hanging on my bedroom wall. I stared at myself for a long moment and then, rather crossly, flung the dress on the bed and opted instead for jeans and a tee shirt. Far more suitable for visiting a stable, I scolded myself. Whatever was I thinking of? There was no way that I wanted to make an impression on any man, least of all on Mr. High and Mighty Bruce. The very last thing I intended to do was get entangled with anyone. Jenny and I are fine as we are, I thought. And we are going to stay that way. I've had enough of men and their selfish ways to last me a life time . . . I pushed my hair back with an impatient hand . . . He is only taking us to see this foal for Jenny's sake and because his mother pushed him into it.

So I gave myself a mental shake and ran down the stairs to join Jenny, who was swinging on the garden gate watching eagerly for Andrew's car.

We didn't have long to wait and as we settled into our seats and fastened the belts, he told us a little of the place and people we were about to meet.

'It's not far,' he said. 'Thompson's farm is in the next village, about four miles away. Bill and Ruth and I practically all grew up together and we've all been what my mother calls 'horse-mad' for as long as I can remember. I don't really get much time for riding these days and I don't think Bill does either now that he helps his father to run the farm. Ruth does though, especially since she has taken up show-jumping.'

He concentrated briefly on manoeuvring the car past a tractor in the narrow lane, giving the driver a cheery wave as he edged past and then continued.

'Ma said you were 'horse-mad' too?'

I answered the question in his voice.

'Well, I suppose you could call it that. At least, I used to be. I learnt to ride when I was little and lived with my Aunt Maggie and she always encouraged it. She bought me my first pony and then gave me Ladybird. She was the sweetest natured little mare . . . about fourteen hands . . . When I left college and . . . and got married, I had hoped to keep them both. There were stables nearby. But it . . . it . . . ' my voice faltered. 'well . . . it just wasn't possible. Then Jenny came along,' I turned my head to smile at her, 'and I was much too busy.'

Briefly my thoughts touched on how Jimmy had always managed to put obstacles in my path when I spoke of my beloved horses.

'I suppose you think you're 'County',' he had said once, sneeringly. 'Better than us 'Townies'.'

Almost as if he had been jealous. He had put pressure on me to sell them and, at last, to keep the peace I had. Once I had made sure that they would have a good home. I remembered how I had shed bitter secretive tears at the time.

I shrugged away such unproductive thoughts and although I felt, rather than saw, Andrew give me a keen glance at my silence, he made no comment.

Andrew drove through the next village and on to the outskirts, turning the car into a side lane and up to a large brick and flint farmhouse. It was obviously old but well cared for and as we drove round to the stable block at the back I noticed how immaculate those buildings were.

As we pulled up, several inquisitive equine heads turned to quiz us, reaching out over half open stable doors with ears pricked forward.

Andrew turned and looked at me with laughter lurking in his eyes.

'Go on,' he said. 'I know you just can't wait to get out there.'

I needed no second invitation and

Jenny and I scrambled out of the car and walked over to the first stable door. I lifted her up and straddled her on my hip and we gently stroked the velvety nose that pushed against us questingly. This one was an old fellow and his wise, kind eyes looked at us with trust as he dropped his tongue into my outstretched hand.

'He wants something to eat, Mummy,' whispered Jenny.

'No, love. That's just his way of being friendly. My pony used to do the same.'

'I know. He's tasting you . . . To see what you're like.'

I laughed at her instinctive understanding and was just about to move on to the next door when a long, low whistle made me whirl around.

Andrew was leaning on the car roof, watching us but another man of about the same age had joined him and I knew without doubt that the wolf whistle had come from him. He spoke in a low voice but I heard him quite clearly.

'School teacher did you say? Why didn't we have them like that when we were at school, old son?'

He was looking at us with such undisguised admiration that I felt my cheeks grow warm. Although he was dressed for farm work in old faded jeans and wellies and a checked work shirt, there was no mistaking his easy air of authority and I guessed him to be Andrew's friend, Bill Thompson. He was fair haired and, although slightly shorter than Andrew, was quite whistle-worthy himself.

Good-looking . . . and knows it, I thought with some amusement, noting the slight swagger and appraising grin as Andrew brought him over to meet me.

After introductions Bill took us to inspect the new foal and Jenny's delight was made complete when she was allowed to stroke its small soft nose. The mare whickered anxiously and I warmed to Bill as he soothed her and I saw his undeniable affection for her.

'She's the only one that's mine now,' he said, fondling the mare's ears. 'All the others belong to my sister, Ruth. She's a good old girl.'

He grinned across at me, showing even white teeth.

'The horse, I mean . . . although my sister's not bad, either!'

We walked back into the yard and, as if on cue, a girl came out of the house towards us.

A slim but curvaceous girl with a mane of riotous curls. Where Bill's hair was sandy, hers was a glorious coppery red and although she had the same classical good looks they were enhanced with faultless make-up. She was dressed in immaculate riding breeches with highly polished boots the colour of old chestnuts and a silk shirt that I knew must have cost the earth. In comparison, I felt like something the cat had brought in . . . and then discarded.

Her gaze flickered over me dismissively and she focussed all her attention on Andrew.

'Andy, darling, why didn't you come in, last time you were here? I looked for you,' she pouted prettily with luscious red lips and, linking her arm with his, snuggled up to him. Then, narrowing her eyes slightly, she looked across at me and said sweetly, 'Well, introduce me then,'

He looked down at her and smiled and gently disengaged himself before making us known to each other but, although her handshake seemed warm, I was disconcerted by a flash of spite that showed for a brief instant in her eyes.

We chatted for a while longer and then Andrew, looking apologetically at his watch, said we would really have to go as he had other calls to make.

'Hang on.' Bill laid his arm casually round my shoulders. 'You're not going to bring this lovely lady into my life and then whisk her away the next minute. Emma can stay longer if she wants and you go off on your calls. I'll see she gets home.'

'Well, certainly . . . If that's what you would like, Emma?' He turned to me and his voice seemed constrained.

'Oh . . . well . . . really that's very nice of you, Bill but . . . ' and I quickly cast around in my mind for an excuse, thankfully remembering . . . I'm afraid I have to get back. I am expecting Pat Somers to come round shortly.'

This was no less than the truth although perhaps the 'shortly' was a slight exaggeration. She was coming to tea.

I moved away from his encircling arm, turning to Andrew as a thought struck me.

'It won't be inconvenient for you to take me back, will it? I mean . . . if you've got calls to make?'

'No, no. I have to go that way, anyway,' and he smiled down at me with no constraint at all.

I think that must have been the first time I had seen him smile so freely and the effect was devastating. I made a dive for the car and took my time fussing with Jenny's seat belt and fiddling with my own. By the time Andrew took his place behind the wheel I had got myself under control and waved cheerfully to Bill and Ruth.

Bill leaned down and spoke through my half-open window.

'I'll see you again, no doubt, Emma. We're having a barbecue some time soon. Will you come?'

'Why, thank you but it depends,' I answered. 'I'll see.' and I waved again as the car shot forward.

On the way back, Andrew told me about the Thompsons, saying amongst other things that Ruth was still very young in some ways.

'And a bit spoilt, too,' he added. 'Understandable I suppose. Her mother died eight years ago when Ruth was only eleven and both her brother and her father dote on her and give her just about everything she wants.'

I made some non-committal remark but thought, bleakly, that she had made it quite plain to me that Andrew was the next desire on her list. Although it shouldn't have mattered to me at all if some young gorgeous thing was setting her cap at him. Sitting at his side, in the closeness of the car, I was acutely aware of his broad-shouldered physique. His masculinity disturbed me in a way I had never known before. Despairingly I knew that Ruth's attempted possessiveness did matter to me . . . far more than it should.

What on earth is wrong with me? I asked myself. I hardly know the man. The first time we met we hardly exchanged a word and the second time all the words were harsh. This is the first time we have spent a few moments together in harmony and . . . and . . . I'm behaving like a moon-struck teenager. I just don't believe this.

I had been looking straight ahead but now my gaze shifted and, as I looked down, my eyes lingered on his hands on the steering wheel. Strong tanned hands with long sensitive fingers. My wayward imagination began to go where it had absolutely no business to go and a little shiver made itself felt deep within me.

I glanced sideways at him as he concentrated on the road ahead and, as if he had felt my gaze, he turned and gave me a smile of such warmth and sweetness that my heart turned over. I felt my cheeks go fiery as I smiled back uncertainly and a feeling of panic gripped me. He mustn't get an inkling of how I am feeling, I thought . . . not for a second. I dipped my head so that my hair swung forward and shielded my face, only to sit up straight again the next second as Andrew gave a shout of laughter.

'I never thought to see that in this day and age!'

I turned towards him warily. 'What?'

'You blushed!' he teased

My hands flew to my face. 'I did no such thing.' I retorted indignantly and, thankfully my moment of alarm fled.

When we stopped outside the school house, Andrew turned towards me.

'I wonder . . . ' he said and then stopped.

I looked at him enquiringly.

'I wonder, would you like to try your hand at riding again? Tomorrow, perhaps? My old fellow has been eating his head off in idleness lately. The exercise would do him good and I know where I can borrow a nice little mare for you. I realise that you haven't ridden for a while but it will soon come back to you. What do you say?'

I was struck dumb with surprise at first and then I found myself clasping my hands together.

'Oh, I don't know what to say. I'd love to but . . . '

Before I could say any more, he broke in.

'Jenny could spend the afternoon with my mother, if she'd like to.'

It was Jenny's turn to clasp her hands together then, in unconscious imitation.

'Oh, please. Could I ride the donkey again?'

'I should think old Moke will be

delighted to oblige.' Andrew answered, solemnly.

He turned back to me.

'Two o'clock?' he asked and I nodded happily, all my previous disquiet vanishing before the thought of the enjoyment ahead. I'm sure I must have had stars in my eyes.

The look he gave me then was strange and still. He reached out his hand.

'Emma . . . '

But I got hurriedly out of the car, not trusting myself.

'See you Sunday, then,' I said brightly. 'And thanks for everything.'

Hand in hand, Jenny and I ran up the path. Jenny to console her beloved Tabitha for being left alone and I . . . well . . . I to seek sanctuary in my little house.

There was no sanctuary from my heart and mind. I stood at my bedroom window and stared out unseeingly. I told myself adamantly that there was no such thing as love at first sight, That it just wasn't possible to care for someone so deeply and irrevocably when you hardly knew them, that it was just a bit of foolish physical attraction and the sooner I stopped it the better.

But it was all to no avail. I sadly had to admit that with no good reasons whatsoever I had fallen in love with Andrew Bruce.

This self-knowledge brought me sadness because I was certain that Andrew had no feelings for me at all. I was also quite sure . . . wasn't I? . . . that there was no way that I was going to enter into a serious relationship of any kind with another man. No matter how devastatingly attractive he may be. I had burnt my fingers once. Only a fool would play with fire a second time. Friendship, yes . . . but nothing more.

There was one thing I was more than positive about. He must never know . . . never even notice a glimmer . . . of my feelings.

Once I had faced up to this problem

I was able to control it. I schooled myself to meet Andrew at all times with impartial friendship and he appeared to take his cue from me. If at times I still longed for more, I kept it to myself.

True to his word he found a sweet-tempered little mare for me. It belonged to a daughter of another farmer friend of his who had gone off to college. For the time being the horse, Dolly, was in great need of exercise which suited us both. When Andrew had the opportunity he rode with me on his rangy cob, Major and there followed a time of halcyon days as we explored the country lanes and byways and the woodland bridle paths. Our friendship flourished . . . perhaps in spite of ourselves.

Other friendships flourished too. Pat and I often spent time together. She helped me tremendously in the garden and there were always village functions and activities to share. We ran the cake stall together at the village fete, knocked on doors to collect jumble for a fundraising effort and joined in whatever was going on. She was indefatigable and swept me along with her.

Bill Thompson wasn't backward in coming forward either. Only a few days after our visit to his home I answered a knock on the door to find him standing there, grinning confidently.

'Evening, Emma. How are you?' He tilted his head and looked down at me with a disarming smile and laughing eyes. 'Not that I need to ask. You look blooming.'

His smile was infectious and I found myself returning it but I recognised the look in his eyes for what it was. A little flirtation was what this young man was looking for. But I was only human and his admiration was warming.

'Why, hello Bill.' I looked at him enquiringly.

'Aren't you going to ask me in?' he said, lazily. 'I've got an invitation for you.'

'Er . . . oh . . . yes, of course. Come

in,' and I led the way to my small sitting room.

He looked around and whistled appreciatively.

'My word! You've made this very nice, Emma. It's certainly different from the last time I saw it. I've heard how hard you've been working. Very busy with the paint pots, I believe.'

He looked at me with a straight face but with a mischievous twinkle in his eyes and I gave an exasperated laugh.

'Oh, don't! Does all the world know about that . . . that accident? I'm trying to forget it.'

'News travels fast around here,' he said solemnly. 'Poor old Andy had a pink face in more ways than one. Anyway, forgotten it shall be. I came to ask you over to our barbecue, Emma. Will you come?'

'When is it?'

'Next Saturday. Practically all our village and half this one will be there. We start about six thirty and go on until the early hours. That's what usually happens. I'll come and pick you up.'

It was quite clear that he was used to having his own way but I had no intention of being bulldozed and explained that first of all I would have to arrange for someone to look after Jenny and then I would let him know. But I thanked him eagerly for it sounded fun. I hadn't been to a barbecue since I was in my teens.

He stayed for coffee and I was beginning to wonder if I was ever going to get rid of him when Jenny called out from her bedroom.

'I shall have to go up to her,' I said. 'Maybe she's had a bad dream,' and I stood up and waited.

He took the hint and moved to go, saying as I opened the door for him

'Give me a ring soon, won't you?'

'Yes, I will. I'll find your number in the telephone book. Goodnight, now.' and I shut the door on him firmly, wondering how soon it would be all over the village that I entertained personable young men in the evenings.

I ran up the stairs to Jenny but she lay, rosily, fast asleep . . . as I had been sure she would. Her voice had only been a sleepy murmur.

I mentioned the barbecue to Pat the next day and she clapped her hands.

'Why, that's great, Emma. Bob and I are going and you can go with us. I'm sure Dora Parfitt will babysit for you.'

When I asked her, Dora was only too pleased and so it was all arranged. Pat had warned me that it would only be casual clothes so Saturday evening saw me dressed in a swirly denim skirt topped with a fresh blue gingham shirt and my hair newly washed and brushed into long loose curls. I felt this was casual but a bit more dressy than jeans and a tee shirt and hoped I was hitting the right note.

The three of us arrived just before seven and Thompson's big barn was already filled with people. Johnny Cash's distinctive voice was coming from a music system somewhere, loud and clear and the smell of frying onions and sausages wafted towards us.

Bill Thompson detached himself from a group of noisy young people and came over to greet us.

'I could have come to fetch you,' he said, reproachfully, 'but never mind, I'll take you home when this shindig is finally over.'

Oh, no, you won't. I thought to myself but merely laughed and made some noncommittal remark, giving Pat a meaning look at the same time.

'We won't mind,' she whispered.

'Maybe not . . . but I will.' I whispered back. 'Don't you dare go home without me.'

A queue of people were waiting by the sizzling barbecue so we opted for drinks from the makeshift bar and I soon found myself in a crowd of friendly young people and started to enjoy myself in a way that I had almost forgotten. The music started up again and Bill pulled me on to the open space in the middle of the barn to join in the line dancing.

'I can't do this,' I gasped, laughing.

'It's a piece of cake,' was the answer. 'Just watch the one in front of you.'

When my feet got hopelessly tangled and I was helpless with laughter and would have beaten a retreat, Bill came up behind me and locked his arms round my waist.

'Now, stick with me, wench and you can't go wrong.'

One of his pals behind us hooted.

'Huh! Stick with him, Emma and you're sure to go wrong!'

It was while we were all fooling about and I was having a fit of the giggles that Andrew strolled in. I had just mastered the first steps of this line dancing but as soon as I saw him my concentration disappeared and I tripped and nearly sent Bill to the floor. Andrew looked across at us and once again that cold set look, that I had tried to forget, was on his face.

I felt a sudden surge of resentment. I'm having fun, I thought. Why shouldn't I laugh and be a bit giddy now and then? I'm still only twenty eight and I don't have to be a stuffy school-marm all the time. I turned away from him and put a bit more energy into my footwork, joining in with all the 'Yee-hahs'.

When the music stopped we were all breathless and Bill swept me across to the bar again, to where Andrew was talking to Pat and Bob.

'Hi, Andy. Glad you could make it. You should have been on the floor with us. This girl's a natural.'

'Not really my thing, old son. I've only come for the burgers.'

He nodded to me briefly and then buried his face in his glass.

My vexation had long since gone and a feeling of desolation was beginning to creep into its place when there was a stir in the people around us and Ruth Thompson made her entrance. It was definitely an entrance, for she outshone every female there.

She was Annie Oakley to the life and her outfit, made of soft, creamy suede, fitted like a second skin, the fringes on her jacket and the short skirt swinging with her every movement. Highly polished cowboy boots showed off long tanned legs and a cream suede Stetson completed the effect. She took off her hat and waved it at us and as she sauntered across the empty floor there wasn't a man there who didn't give her a glance of appreciation.

'Hi, Pat . . . Bob. Oh, hello, Emma. Didn't see you at first.' She nodded casually and made a bee-line for Andrew.

'Andy, darling. I knew you wouldn't let me down.' She clung to him, possessively and reached up to nibble his ear.

'For goodness sake, Ruth.' He gave an embarrassed laugh but didn't attempt to pull away. 'What will you have to drink? A St. Clements? That's your favourite, isn't it?'

She pouted prettily.

'Oh, Andy, no. I'll have a g. and t. please.'

'Not from me you won't.' His voice

was firm and he turned away to give the order.

Her brother snorted with laughter.

'You won't get round old Andy so easily, Ruthie.'

'Shut up, Bill,' she glared at him and then schooled her features as Andrew turned back to us with her drink in his hand.

'It's so hot in here, Darling. Let's take our drinks outside.'

'That's a good idea,' chipped in Pat. 'Let's all go out,' and she swept us all before her, apparently oblivious of Ruth's dagger-like looks. But although we were in a group, Ruth monopolised Andrew all evening and he made no move away from her. Not in my direction anyway.

We listened to some more country and western music and danced again. The food was good although I had little appetite for it. Ruth dragged Andrew off on some pretext to do with her horses and we didn't see them again and all I wanted to do was go home.

The general din was escalating and the stuffiness in the barn and all-pervading smell of frying onions combined to give me the beginnings of a headache.

Determined that no-one should guess how I felt, I was probably more animated than I should have been and probably only had myself to blame when Bill whirled me outside into the darkness after a hectic bit of jive and pulled me into his arms.

'I've been wanting to do this all night,' he murmured huskily and reached for my mouth.

'No, Bill.' I pushed against his shoulders with all my strength and wriggled free.

'Oh, come on, Emma. Be good to me.'

'No way. Behave yourself, Bill,' and I marched back into the barn with my cheeks flaming.

Fortunately the lights were low and there was such a haze that no-one noticed us either go out or come back in but I felt it was time to go home and sought out Pat and Bob. Pat greeted me with relief.

'I was just coming to look for you. I hate to tear you away when you seem to be having such a good time.'

'Oh, I'm more than ready to go home, Pat.'

Bill caught up with us and held me back for a moment.

'You're not going because of me, are you?'

'No, of course not, Bill. Pat and Bob are ready for going home, that's all.'

'Let them go then. I'll run you home later.'

But I had had enough and I explained that Mrs. Parfitt would be waiting for me.

'Friends, Emma?'

'Of course.'

He wasn't the sort to feel any kind of rebuff and before I could avoid him he bent and kissed me swiftly.

'Gotcha!' he said and his teeth gleamed in the darkness. 'I'll see you again . . . and soon.'

The next time I went over to the field behind Croxfield Hall to saddle up the little mare I was prepared for Andrew to be cold and unfriendly again or even not to be there. But I was wrong. He had already saddled Major and came across to lend me a hand with Dolly. I told myself that I had imagined his disapproval, the night of the barbecue and greeted him thankfully, just glad he was there. The memory of him walking away with Ruth that night I banished from my mind. Anyway, if I was realistic, it was nothing to do with me.

So the days passed swiftly and my life was busy, full of growing friendships and fulfilling work. My contentment flourished on the whole and if, now and then, I felt a certain restlessness and a sense of something vital missing from my life, then I kept those feelings firmly at the back of my mind.

They were good days.

I remember saying to Peggy, long afterwards, that those few weeks were such golden ones and I gained so much from them. It had almost been as if the fates were allowing me to build up reserves of strength and confidence.

Just once ... and I can't really remember why ... I had a kind of premonition on a particularly happy day, when a flash of fear at so much blessedness had struck me. It was almost as if I had been given a warning of trouble ahead. I little knew, then, just what black trouble it was going to be.

6

The Summer term continued through weeks of sunshine and I was happy and content. I enjoyed my work and my children soon settled into what I hoped was a disciplined but enjoyable routine.

Only George remained a thorn in everyone's side. However, I felt that I must have been getting through to him in some way when one afternoon, at the end of school, his mother, Mrs. Pegg came along to speak to Douglas on some matter and stopped to have a word with me. She was a thin, dispirited looking woman with lank brown hair straggling over the drooping neck of an old grey cardigan and wearing a shapeless cotton skirt that had seen better days long ago.

'I wus hopin' I might see you, Miss.'

I eyed her warily. What mischief had George been up to now?

'Hello, Mrs. Pegg. What can I do for you?'

'Oh, nuthin', Miss. I just wanted to tell yer that our George hen't been half as bad since you come.'

She laid a work-worn hand on my arm.

'I'm ever so grateful and so's his dad. Everyone used to pick on 'im suthin cruel and he wus allus gettin' wrong an playin' hookey. I never could do nuthin' with 'im. But he don't miss school no more now an' he's gettin' ter be a diff'rent boy.'

I covered her hand with mine and smiled at her.

'George is a bright boy. Once he realises this and puts his mind to school work instead of mischief, he'll be fine.'

She brightened and pushed her straggly hair behind her ears.

'Oh, I allus knew he had it in 'im, Miss,' and she nodded and hurried off in the direction of Douglas's office, her shoulders a little straighter than before.

I watched her go and wondered if all

the tales I had heard about her shifty husband were true. If they were to be believed, he was not above using violence on her or their brood of children and he certainly wasn't much of a provider. I sighed and turned back to my desk, thinking that it was going to be an uphill struggle with her eldest, even if he was bright.

Duncan, my little handicapped boy, was waiting patiently for his mother to collect him and I held out my hand.

'Mummy will be here soon, Duncan.'

He leaned against me, trustingly, his pale, china-blue eyes fixed on my face and a wide grin illuminating his chubby features.

'Where's your hanky, love?'

I bent over him, wiping his face gently. 'There's a good boy. Go and get your number bricks out of the cupboard while you are waiting.'

I gave him a quick hug and sent him on his way. He was such an affectionate child but not as teachable as the little Down's Syndrome girl who had been in my care at Norton, my last school. Apparently there were other health problems and Douglas had warned me that his future was precarious.

'Apart from that,' he had added, 'his mother is a most feckless young woman. I doubt very much whether she even knows who Duncan's father is! She idolises that little boy but has no idea of how to look after him. He is for ever wandering about the village and fields and if the other children didn't look out for him as they do, he might very well come to harm, for he has no idea of self preservation. Why, just before you came here, he went missing and was found up to his waist in the old marl pit. Trying to catch a moorhen, if you please!'

I heard the clack of high heels and Duncan's mother arrived breathlessly. Late as usual and full of excuses. She made a colourful entrance in her tight orange skirt, even shorter than usual and a fluffy purple jumper and rushed over to pick Duncan up and hug him.

'Here we are, Dunky boy. Let's be off then. Ta-ra, Miss.'

I saw them out and at last was able to close the door on my classroom and go home.

My friendship with Pat Somers had flourished and we were finding much in common but some of my happiest times were spent in riding the little mare that Andrew had borrowed for me, exploring the country lanes and woodland paths. The farmer who owned Dolly had been only too pleased for Andrew to keep her in the field where his own cob, Major, lived and at weekends Andrew and I rode off together, spending more and more time in each other's company. Jenny revelled in the loving attentions of her 'Auntie Gwen' and rode Old Moke to her heart's content. As I came to know Andrew better, I began to lose my feeling of wariness and realised that my first impressions of his character had been arrived at too hastily. In his dealings with the animals in his care, his relationship with his parents and friends and his growing rapport with me, I saw him to be a man of integrity and sensitivity. I noticed how Jenny appeared to place complete trust in him and had taken to calling him. 'Uncle Andrew' and that influenced me even more.

I was still puzzled about the antagonism I had encountered at our first meeting but had come to the conclusion that it might have something to do with my apparent likeness to his one-time girlfriend. That is, if Dora was to be believed. Anyway, our friendship was too new for me to start questioning him about this and, thinking it was best to let sleeping dogs lie, I gave it no more thought. I found myself looking forward to those weekend rides more and more and my earlier caution was fast disappearing in a puff of euphoria.

One Saturday, Andrew had taken the day off and we had ridden further afield than usual. We stopped by a riverside to give the horses and ourselves a much needed breather. As Major and Dolly dropped their heads to the grass with every appearance of enjoyment, Andrew flung himself down on to the wide grassy bank and held out his hand to me.

I avoided his hand but sat down next to him. I was hot and flushed after our last canter and my fingers were strangely clumsy as I tried to unfasten my helmet.

'Hold still,' he said. 'Let me.' And he impatiently shook off his own hat and then, oh, so gently, undid my straps and released me, only to imprison me again with his hands cradling my face. A shiver ran right through me at the touch of his fingers and I forgot all my caution and all my resolutions and offered no resistance at all as he pulled me slowly forwards until our mouths touched. The kiss that started so tenderly changed to fire and passion within moments and when at last we surfaced we were both breathless.

Muttering my name deep in his

throat, he reached for me again and I went to him so very willingly, my arms finding their way around his neck of their own volition and my fingers threading through his thick and springy hair. Oh, but this was what I had been longing for. It felt so right . . . so good. His arms came round me as if they would never let me go and we sank back on the lush grass. I felt my innermost self whirling and dizzying beyond belief. Any defences I might have had disappeared under the touch and warmth of his mouth on mine as he kissed me again, deeply and searchingly. I kissed him back with equal abandon, my mouth opening under his insistence. I just closed my eyes . . . and closed my mind . . . and gave in to my urgent need to hold him and be held. How long we lay there, our kisses and caresses growing more and more ardent and demanding, I have no idea. I was only conscious of trembling delight as his strong hands caressed me and I arched towards him with a longing that seemed to fill my whole body. A longing that I knew I had never, ever felt before and which was robbing me of almost every last vestige of caution. It was only when I felt his hand at my waist, seeking and exploring and was suddenly, shockingly, aware of an answering jolt of desire flooding through me, that I came to my senses.

Somehow I managed to place my shaking hands against his chest and push myself away.

'Andrew . . . no . . . no.' My voice was a thread but I gasped a deep and choking breath and it grew stronger.

'No . . . I . . . we . . . ' I was lost and confused.

He slowly released me and I sat up hurriedly and pushed back my hair with unsteady fingers. I couldn't look at him.

He levered himself up beside me and reached out to tuck a stray tendril of hair behind my ear.

'Oh, Emma, don't be upset. I'm sorry if I pushed my luck. I guess we got caried away.' His voice was ragged.

Then, as I turned towards him, it softened.

'I'm not going to apologise for kissing you. You might as well know, I've been wanting to do that for quite some time.'

I caught a glimmer in his eyes and he looked at me intently.

'Don't tell me that you didn't enjoy it as much as I did?'

I shook my head helplessly but I knew I had to be honest with him.

'No, I won't. You must have known what I felt. But . . . but please, Andrew let's take things a little slower. I . . . I'm not sure . . . '

My voice tailed away. I couldn't remember when I had last felt so at a loss for words. So desperately unsure of myself.

He looked at me for a long moment and his face was sombre but then he smiled and a surge of relief filled my heart.

'Alright, if that's what you want, Emma.'

With one lithe movement he was on

his feet and holding out a hand. I let him help me up and as I looked up at him he let go of my hand and laid his own against my cheek, stroking his thumb sensuously across my still trembling lips. Those keen dark eyes looked down, searchingly, into mine and I don't know what he saw there but it took every bit of my slowly returning willpower to stop myself from flinging my arms around his neck again. I forced myself to stay still under his gentle touch and he gave an almost imperceptible shrug and smiled again and his hands slid to my shoulders.

'I can wait,' he spoke quietly and then in a louder voice, 'Come on then, let's put a stop to those greedy beggars before they get too blown out to take us home,' and he turned to the grazing horses.

I knew only too well that it wasn't what I wanted at all. A flame had been lit inside me and I longed to feel his arms around me again, holding me close. Yet I was sure . . . wasn't I?

. . . that such longings would only lead to disillusion in the end. I valued the friendship that was blossoming between us and I was wary of doing anything that might spoil this. Yet I hungered for more. The thought of sharing the intimacies of love with this man filled me with such a desperate yearning that my whole body trembled again. But it was too soon. Much too soon.

I grabbed my hat, crammed it on my head and swung myself up into the saddle, fearful of Andrew sensing my feelings.

'Race you to the road,' I shouted over my shoulder and took off as if the devil was at my heels. Which, in a way, he was.

When we pulled up at the roadside, both of us were breathless and laughing and the moments of tension were gone.

As we neared the village and slowed the horses down to a walk, Andrew asked me if I had any plans about going to the Norfolk Show which would be taking place in a few days time.

'I'll take you and Jenny if you like. I shall be the duty vet but I may only have to be on call and we can make a day of it. What do you say?'

'Oh, yes. That would be lovely.' I was delighted. 'We get two days off school because of the Show and I was wondering if I would be able to take Jenny on the bus. I'd heard there would be specials that go round the villages.'

'Of course, if you'd rather go by bus.' He put on a mock injured air and on a note of laughter we made plans for the outing.

'Dress comfortably,' Andrew warned. 'None of this high heels and fancy hat nonsense . . . and we'll take a picnic.'

'I'll see to that.' I offered quickly but he looked across at me and grinned.

'No need. That's all been taken care of. All you have to do is enjoy yourself.'

I chuckled. 'Sure of yourself, weren't you. Such cheek!' I felt as young and as carefree as a teenager again.

As I followed Andrew into Croxfield Hall's driveway I glanced up the street and noticed a dashing blue and silver sports car parked a short way further along. I barely had time to see its driver before the car exploded into action and roared past behind me and away out of the village, causing my gentle little mare to rear up in alarm, ears back and eyes rolling wildly. It was so unexpected that I only just managed to stay in the saddle and Andrew turned sharply.

'What the devil . . . Emma, are you alright? Who on earth was that fool?'

'I'm fine.' I answered, reaching down to pat and soothe Dolly. 'It was just someone in a hurry, that's all.'

'Ought to have more sense,' he said tersely but left it at that.

The one in a hurry had been Ruth Thompson. Those flaming curls left no room for doubt. What had shaken me more than my horse's behaviour was the venomous glare she had given me as she roared past. There was no mistaking the anger which prompted it.

I shrugged my shoulders and forgot about it.

The morning of the show arrived with blue skies and that hint of a haze that promises glorious sunshine. I took out my pretty yellow dress and brushed out my hair to curl loosely on my shoulders. As I made up my face with merely a minimum of make-up I stared sternly at myself in the mirror. The face that looked back at me was suntanned and glowing, with sparkling eyes. The small lecture I was about to give myself on wisdom and common sense was forgotten aand I laughed out loud and twirled around. For wasn't I about to spend the day with the man I loved? And maybe . . . just maybe . . . but then Jenny ran in with a sandal in her hand and my dangerous and wilful thoughts subsided.

'Mummy, I can't fasten this.'

She looked adorable in her pale blue dungarees and embroidered tee shirt.

I crouched down to fasten her sandal and we looked into each other's faces and laughed, eyes dancing.

'What fun,' I said. 'Aren't we going to have a lovely time, sweetheart?'

'Rabbits,' said Jenny, dreamily. 'and guinea pigs and goats and baby piglets and lambs and . . . and . . . '

'Oh, yes. All those and more.' I straightened, still laughing and shook the creases from my dress. 'Come along, love. Downstairs with you. Bring your cardi.'

I stood by the door, ready to lock up.

'Jenny, we'd better get down to the gate and be ready.'

'Just a minute.'

She ran to where Jess was sitting expectantly on the hearthrug, her feathery tail beating a tattoo and her ears pricked and gave the dog a hug.

'You can't come, Jess. Mrs. Parfitt is going to look after you and Tabitha. Now just be good while we're out.'

She took my hand and together we quickly went down the path to the old wooden gate.

There was a blue and silver sports car

waiting in the road beyond and, as we approached, Ruth slid out from the driver's seat and stood, leaning negligently against the door.

I felt a moment's apprehension but her expession was enigmatic and I detected no antagonism on her face this time.

'Sorry, Emma, I've got a disappointment for you. Andrew had a sudden call which of course he couldn't ignore. He rang up and asked us to give you a lift in to the show. He'll be along later.'

I hesitated. Why hadn't Andrew called me himself to let me know? I wouldn't have minded waiting.

As if she had divined my thoughts, Ruth walked round the car and held the door open.

'He just didn't have time to ring you. Anyway, he knew we were going. It was all arranged ages ago. Jump in.'

She flashed me a brilliant smile which, somehow, didn't reach her eyes.

I swallowed my deep disappointment and we sqeezed in and on to the small back seat. Was this what Andrew had meant when he said that the picnic was all taken care of? I glanced at Bill who was watching from the front seat with a delighted grin on his face and gave him a small smile.

'My gain,' he said. 'Don't you worry about old Andy. He'll turn up later. Much later, I hope!'

Ruth appeared to be fiddling about with the gate for some reason but then she swung round to get behind the wheel and within seconds we were roaring off towards the Norwich road.

As we turned on to the main road, Bill looked across at Ruth and complained.

'I wish you'd called me when Andy phoned. When did he ring? I wanted to have a word with him about the mare.'

Ruth didn't answer at first but concentrated on passing a lorry and giving the driver a blare on her horn. Then she shrugged and answered curtly.

'How was I supposed to know that?

Anyway, you weren't anywhere about. You'll see him at the grandstand when he comes to watch me jump.'

Our conversation during the journey was desultory but I learnt that Ruth was competing in the show jumping, although I had guessed as much from her immaculate outfit. It was only natural that Andrew would want to watch her endeavours, for after all they had been friends for a long time but I couldn't help feeling that our lovely day together, which I had been so looking forward to, seemed to be disappearing, bit by bit. Bill also had certain duties but he told me airily that he would have plenty of time to show me round if Andy was late. I made some non-committal answer, hoping very much that Andrew would soon join us.

We joined the queue of cars waiting to go into the showground but Ruth veered off at the gateway to drive to the Member's park and we were soon making our way into the hub of things. She left us with an airy wave of her hand.

'Right. I'm off to see to the horses. See you later, Bill. We've to join Dad for lunch. Don't forget. Remind Andy if you see him.'

Then she turned back as if it were an afterthought.

'Oh, Emma. I expect you'll be able to find yourself a snack somewhere. There are loads of places about.'

I felt my face burn at her cavalier treatment and noticed a frown on Bill's face.

'My sister can forget her manners sometimes, I'm afraid.' he said uncomfortably. 'I'm sure you will be expected to join us all for lunch.'

'Thank you, Bill but Andrew and I had arranged a picnic. Please don't worry about us. Although, . . . ' and here my voice must have betrayed my feelings, ' . . . how he will find us in all this crush, I can't imagine.'

'With the greatest difficulty, I hope.'

and he grinned at me widely, his jauntiness returning immediately. 'Ruth will have fixed something up. Andy won't be here yet awhile and we'll go round to the horse boxes later and have a word with her. In the meantime will you accept me as your escort? At least until Andy gets here. We can't have you two delicious ladies wandering round on your own. Who knows who or what might snap you up?'

He grinned down at Jenny, who giggled happily.

I gave him a wide smile also. I knew he was taking advantage of the situation but I was sure it would only be for a little while. He really was rather nice and it would be churlish to refuse. Andrew would be here soon.

'Thank you, Bill. That's kind of you.' and at Jenny's insistence I allowed myself to be swept away to the animal pens and tents.

Bill was an amusing companion, informative too and the time passed quickly although I was constantly on the lookout for that tall broad-shouldered, dark haired man who had filled most of my waking thoughts lately . . . and many sleeping ones as well.

Jenny was in her seventh heaven, stroking every goat, sheep and piglet within her reach. 'Ohh, Mummy, look!' was her constant cry. We reached the main lane which threaded its way through the centre of the showground and Bill looked at his watch and said, apologetically, 'I have to go and see to a bit of farm business I'm afraid and I shall have to dash. I've left it a bit late. Then I'll go and see what arrangements Ruth has made. Will you meet me back here in an hour's time? Mind you, Andy will probably have arrived by now. Perhaps you'll even bump into him and if you do and you're not here when I come back, that's O.K. Everyone walks up and down these lanes and we'll all see each other from time to time. If I see him first, I'll tell him where you are. Alright?'

I mustered a smile and nodded.

'Yes, thank you, Bill. I'll take Jenny to the fun fair for a little while.'

He looked at me intently and then said, with a mischievous grin,

'I hope you don't mind me saying this, Emma but I hope our Andy doesn't get here at all. He's had you to himself for far too long.'

Before I could protest, his arms went round me and he gave me a quick hug. He would have kissed me as well but I managed to evade him.

'Really, Bill! Behave yourself.'

I couldn't help laughing. His grin was so infectious and I knew it was all done only in fun. I pushed him away and he lifted a hand in salute and was gone.

I put my hand up to my hair and turned, still laughing and there, standing stock still in the middle of the lane, not fifty yards away was Andrew.

I started towards him, feeling a huge relief and gladness but there was no answering pleasure on his face. His features were set and his eyes blazed with a fury that stopped me in my tracks. Without one word he turned and walked away.

He had seen me. There was no doubt about that. Had that silly little incident with Bill upset him? But he knew what Bill was like. Bill had tried to flirt with me on other odd occasions when Andrew and I had met up with him and Andrew knew it meant nothing. Why should it bother him now?

It was a long, long time before I discovered the reason.

I seized Jenny's hand.

'Quickly, love. I thought I saw Uncle Andrew. Let's see if we can catch him up,' and I hurried her along.

I had to find him.

At an intersection the crowd thinned and I looked distractedly both ways. I saw him then, striding grimly towards the Grandstand and quickened my pace but jolted to a stop when Ruth came flying down the Grandstand steps and caught hold of his arm.

He looked down at her as he spoke and then put his arms around her shoulders and they walked off together. Ruth turned her head and for one instant her eyes looked straight into mine and I'll swear there was malicious triumph showing.

Wild horses wouldn't have dragged me after him then.

I turned aimlessly, feeling choked but Jenny's tugging at my hand pulled me round.

'Where is he, Mummy? I can't see him.'

'I was mistaken, love. I expect he's too busy right now. Perhaps . . . perhaps there's another little foal that needs looking after. Or perhaps there's a dog with a hurt leg. Could be, you know.'

My chin went up a notch and I squared my shoulders.

'We'll go and have a look at the fun-fair shall we, poppet? I think there'll be a round-a-bout and I believe there's a funny kind of house that you can go into that has all kinds of wobbly floors and things . . .' and if my voice was was a little wobbly too, at first, she never noticed.

So we spent time at the fun-fair and then headed for the Morris dancers. It was while I was looking at my programme to find the time and place that Ruth suddenly appeared at my side.

'Oh, there you are, Emma. I've got a message for you from Andy. He's finally arrived and he asked me to look out for you and make his apologies. We've been invited to lunch in the committee tent so I'm afraid the picnic's off. Such a shame . . . but one can't offend the powers that be, you know.'

I gritted my teeth but answered quietly enough.

'I quite understand. Tell him not to give it another thought.'

'Oh, and Bill has got to see someone about the new tractor we're getting and won't be able to meet you at the time he planned. If you will be at the Grandstand at one thirty, he'll take you for lunch.'

I shook back my hair and said, coolly, 'That's very kind of him but there's really no need. Jenny and I will find a snack somewhere. Please tell him that would be better.'

But Ruth hadn't finished. She went in for the kill.

'I'm really sorry,' she said sweetly. 'I'm afraid my Andy gets carried away sometimes. He's always one for looking after waifs and strays. He's such a generous person. But then, he's generous to me too, so I can't really complain.'

She lifted her left hand and twisted a magnificent emerald ring which encircled her third finger.

'He doesn't want anyone to know about this just yet but I don't mind telling you,' and she smiled sweetly again.

I bet you don't, I thought bitterly but I looked at her, unswervingly.

'Are congratulations in order, then?'

'All in good time,' she smirked triumphantly . . . but her eyes were watchful as she delivered the coup-de-grace.

'One more thing. We shall all be staying on until quite late, so do you think you could make your own way home? I believe there are plenty of buses.'

'Of course,' I said, between my teeth. 'Don't give it another thought. Come, Jenny,' and I turned and marched us both away. I'd had enough of her and there was no way that I was going to give her the satisfaction of seeing my disappointment and fury.

'Mummy!' protested Jenny, after five minutes of this. 'Go slower. My legs won't keep up.'

'Oh, I am sorry, love.' I was filled with compunction. 'I tell you what, let's go and get an icecream, shall we?'

'Aren't we going to see Uncle Andrew, then?'

'Mr. Bruce, Jenny and no, we are not going to see him.'

I knew my voice was harsh but it was my effort to control my unhappy thoughts that made it so.

'He told me to call him Uncle Andrew.'

quavered a small mutinous voice. 'Are you cross with me, Mummy?'

'No, Darling. Of course not.'

I swept her up in my arms and gave her a fierce hug. I buried my face in her soft curls and took a deep breath. When she pulled her head back to look into my face I was able to smile at her lovingly and reassuringly.

'Now, about that icecream?'

For the rest of the day I concentrated hard on giving my little daughter a happy time but all I wanted for myself was to go home and grieve for lost dreams and foolish hopes.

Spineless! I chided myself. That's what you are, my girl. Ruth's turn of phrase, 'waifs and strays' came to mind and I winced. All he was doing was being kind . . . and from deep within me a bitter voice added . . . and making the most of his opportunities.

After enquiries, I found that we could get home on one of the many coaches that were lined up in the showground park.

'Don't you worry, my woman.' assured the cheery coach driver. 'I'll squeeze you in somehow and get you home.'

Which was precisely what he did and I sat on the one remaining seat with Jenny on my lap and leaned my aching head against the window. The late afternoon sunshine lit up the surrounding countryside with gold as we sped along from village to village but my thoughts were sad and bitter and I saw none of its beauty. There was so much that I found difficult to understand and come to terms with.

7

At last the bus ground to a halt at the crossroads in Little Croxfield. In common with most Norfolk buses, it had travelled through many small villages on its way and I was beginning to think that we were going to end up like the Flying Dutchman . . . doomed to ride on for ever. Jenny was practically asleep on her feet as we clambered off the bus and as we reached the school house, I was only conscious of a huge feeling of relief that I was home at last.

Something puzzled me as I pushed open the wooden gate. A scrap of paper was pinned to the gate post and I could just make out the letters 'Andr . .' Was this what Ruth had been doing just before we set off for the show? Leaving a note for Andrew? But why? She said she had spoken to him on the phone.

I sighed and looked down and caught

sight of a screwed up piece of the same kind of paper lodged in a clump of flowers and, more from a habit of tidiness than anything else, bent down to pick it up and pushed it into my dress pocket. We trailed wearily up to the front door and let ourselves in. Jess's rapturous welcome cheered me and Dora, bless her, had laid the fire all ready for me to put a match to and left a note to say that she had left a meat pie in the oven.

'Oh, goody.' said Jenny, who had a partiality for Dora's meat pies, rich with tender beef and swimming in gravy.

I turned the oven on and put a match to the fire for, although it was far from cold, a glowing, flickering fire can be a great comfort. Feeling thankful for good friends, I stood in the kitchen waiting for the kettle to boil and then remembered the bit of paper I had picked up in the garden. I took it out of my pocket and was just going to drop it in the bin when a thought made me hesitate and I flattened out its creases.

It seemed to be part of a torn up note and the wording on it made no sense at all.

It read, 'It looks

> to be to
> take us t
> Well, no-o
> waiting so
> with Bill in
> E'

I stared at it in bewilderment and then dismissed it with a shake of my head and stuffed it back into my pocket again, meaning to throw it into the fire when it got going. But I forgot it and it stayed in my pocket and went into the linen basket that night when I went to bed.

After the disaster of the Norfolk Show, I immersed myself in my work believing that I only had myself to blame for my unhappiness. Hadn't Andrew himself said, that afternoon by the riverside, that he had got 'carried away'? Obviously that was all it meant to him and I was a fool to think anything different. The one thing I was overwhelmingly thankful for was that I had kept my head. I was uncomfortably aware that if Andrew had kissed me again I might well have matched his desire with my own and given everything of myself, heart and soul.

In my previous marriage, I had loved Jimmy but I now knew that it had been a young immature love. When I was completely honest with myself I also knew that it hadn't survived Jimmy's uncaring attitude and that it had died long before the end of our life together. This feeling I had for Andrew was altogether different. This was fire and passion . . . and tenderness and caring and . . . I was very much afraid . . . was a love that was for ever and ever.

I tried hard to disown it. Infatuation, I told myself, in a vain attempt to deny my emotions. Just a temporary touch of madness. I did my best to ignore it, to stifle it before it could overwhelm me. I even tried to whip up anger against Andrew as a defence. On the whole I was successful but in the dark hours of the night I often tossed and turned. The only way I could cope with this was to tell myself that it had been an instinctive reaction to the attentions of an attractive man combined with just a touch of loneliness. I got carried away too. That's all it was and I'd be stupid to read anything else into it.

I had only seen Andrew once since the fiasco of the show. He had nodded curtly as he passed in his car and I had acknowledged him with equal brevity. It seemed there were going to be no explanations and I wondered sadly just what Ruth must have said to him. Fully aware that she had no liking for me, I was fairly sure that it would have been something to cause a rift in the friendship that had been growing between Andrew and myself. And why not? I admitted wryly to myself that if they were as close as she told me, then I suppose she had every right to do so.

I couldn't really understand just what had gone wrong with that day. I found it difficult to believe that Andrew had been angered at seeing me with Bill. Surely he had known that I would have been waiting for him to turn up? Perhaps I was becoming some sort of embarrassment to him . . . especially if he and Ruth were planning to get engaged.

A couple of days after the show, when I took my yellow dress out of the linen basket to wash it I felt something in the pocket. It was the screwed-up piece of paper I had found by the gate. I smoothed it out on the kitchen table and studied it carefully. I remembered the tiny piece which had still been pinned to the gatepost and this was undoubtedly part of the same note. A note to Andrew. The capital 'E' bothered me. Could it possibly be the beginning of 'Emma'? Could it be that Ruth had left him a note supposedly from me? . . . Telling him that I had gone to the Show with Bill? It certainly seemed to fit and undoubtedly would account for his anger. No man likes to be stood up. I considered the possibility and then discarded it as being too far-fetched. Why, surely she wouldn't do a thing like that . . . would she? I shook my head at myself angrily. I was being stupid. It must have been a note for Andrew but just to tell him that she had picked me up as arranged. I was getting paranoid and I didn't like the feeling. He's not for you, my girl. I told myself. Forget it.

But for some unaccountable reason I pushed the scrap of paper into the kitchen drawer where I kept all my odd bits and pieces.

The days passed and I found, as I had done in the past, that school was one of the best places to be in if I had any worries to contend with. For I just didn't have a moment's time in which to think about them. This was especially true at the end of term and even more so at the end of the summer term. With so much extra paperwork to get through and assessments to make, I was fully occupied. To add to this, the highlight of our coming Sports Day was driving all thoughts of work or rational behaviour out of every child's head.

Every spare minute they had, either in or out of school, was spent in practising races or jumps or in staggering round the playground in twos, legs tied together with woolly scarves or belts. Even Jenny caught the fever and rehearsed the egg and spoon race in a distinctly wobbly fashion around the kitchen with eggs purloined from the fridge. Jess joined in with enthusiasm, especially when the egg landed on the floor. Coming into the kitchen after the third attempt, I had to call a halt and consoled her with a hug, hiding my smiles in her curls.

'Never mind, sweetheart. When you run in the race on Sports day you won't have to use a real egg and it won't break, I promise you.'

Nearly every one who was home in the village wandered up to the playing field at the beginning of that all-important afternoon, some of them bringing their own chairs and even picnic baskets. Family groups settled themselves in strategic positions and spread themselves and their debris about. Toddlers and babies got under everyone's feet, bottles of pop were brought out and the latest village gossip was bandied from one circle to another.

The school children in their shorts and tee shirts rushed about, full of self importance, getting in the wrong groups, losing the numbers they were supposed to have pinned on their backs, generally creating mayhem . . . and inciting their teachers to pleasurable thoughts of murder.

I thought back to the high-powered and extremely well organised Sports days I had been involved with during my career in Manchester and grinned to myself as I hurried over to Catherine who was fighting a losing battle with George and the finishing tape.

'George Pegg!' I spoke as severely as

I could. 'You are not to move that tape. Leave it alone.'

'Aw, Miss.' He beamed at me with an innocent smile but with a devil lurking at the back of his eyes. 'It weren't fair. Li'l ole Billy shouldn't ha' won. He started afore any o' them others. I wus only givin' them others a chance.'

'Those others,' I corrected automatically and shepherded him out of harm's way, trying desperately to control the twitch at the corner of my mouth. 'Isn't it nearly time for the sack race? I know you've been practising. How about if you go and fetch the sacks from my classroom? Find someone sensible to help you.'

And George bustled off, full of importance and good intentions.

With the combined efforts of staff and a few willing parents, order triumphed over threatened chaos and races were run and records were broken, to the great satisfaction of the winners. There was great hilarity and shouts of encouragement during the parents' races, a vast amount of squash and coke was consumed, a few tears mopped up and a good time was had by all.

'We'll clear up the field in the morning.' Douglas mopped his forehead. 'I feel as if I've been put through the wringer and I'm sure you both feel the same.'

'That must be the understatement of the year.' I rolled my eyes heavenwards and Catherine allowed herself a slightly more than prim smile.

The rest of the week passed in a flurry of end-of-term sorting and packing until, at last, all work was finished and the classrooms had become bare and unfamiliar places. The children straggled home clutching an assortment of precious handiwork and paintings, shoe-bags and sports kits and after we had all made our goodbyes I trailed across to the school house to kick off my shoes and collapse into my armchair. Much as I had enjoyed my first term, the thought of the long summer holiday ahead was blissful.

Jenny climbed onto my lap still carefully holding her pride and joy . . . a slightly creased painting of a house surrounded by a variety of quite recognisable animals. They were all there. Jess, Tabitha, Old Moke and even the dog with bandages on his leg. A peculiar creature sat on top of the roof which puzzled me until Jenny explained that it was one of the school rabbits and there hadn't been room to put it anywhere else.

'Ah,' I said. 'Of course. And where shall we put this masterpiece?'

'On the wall, of course. Will you pin it up now, Mummy?'

'I think I'd better,' I agreed. 'Before we get more paint on us than there is on your picture.'

We looked at each other and laughed for the poster paint had rubbed off on to both our faces.

'We're like Red Indians,' giggled Jenny and an echoing giggle sounded from the open doorway. Pat Somers stood there surveying us both with amusement.

'You're right, Jenny. All you need are a few feathers in your hair. I'll bring you some back from Canada.'

She grinned widely at me as I lay sprawled in my chair.

'My! Aren't you the relaxed one. Any chance of a cuppa?'

'I should think so. If you put the kettle on, pal, I'll make one in a minute.'

'I'm sorry to barge in on you like this when you've only just got home but I wanted to ask you a favour.'

'Ask away then.'

She turned back into the kitchen and switched the kettle on before coming to sit down opposite us.

'We leave on Thursday as you know. If I give you a key, will you pop in from time to time and keep an eye on my plants indoors? Ada, next door was going to do it but at the last minute decided to go and stay with her sister for a couple of weeks. I really would be grateful.'

'Of course I will. I'll pick up your mail as well.'

'Mmm. Thanks, love.'

'I shall really miss you, you know.'

'Go on! You'll be far too busy riding round the countryside with our dashing Andrew to miss me.'

She looked across at me with a sly grin and I did my best to grin back at her as if her supposition were true. I saw no point in telling anyone of the rift that was widening between Andrew and myself.

'You're going to be away for most of the school holidays, aren't you?'

'Well, if we're going to go all that way to Canada, we might as well make the most of it. I'll send you postcards but it will be no use you trying to write back. We're going to be travelling from place to place visiting all the relatives there.'

'Lucky old you! I do hope you have a lovely time.'

I got up to make the tea and Pat called after me.

'Save all the news for when I get back,' and then added, 'not that there will be much to tell from this sleepy little place. Nothing ever happens here.'

Many weeks later she was to remember those words and shake her head in disbelief.

Gwen Bruce knocked at my door one morning during the first week of the holidays.

'Where have you been? We haven't seen you or Jenny for ages'

'Do come in, Gwen. Coffee?' I felt myself flush, feeling guilty at my neglect of these good friends. 'Go and sit down and I'll put the kettle on.'

'Lovely. Thanks.' She went through into the sitting room and then turned and put her head on one side and looked at me quizzically. 'You've lost weight,' she said, bluntly. 'Have you found your first term hard going?'

'Oh, no,' I assured her. 'It's been great, although I must admit the last few weeks have been extremely busy and I'm glad the holidays are here.'

I felt my face grow warmer still as she continued.

'Forgive me, my dear, if I seem to be

interfering but it's something to do with Andrew, isn't it? He's been like a bear with a sore head just lately.' She gave a small sigh. 'I thought you two were getting on so well.'

I backed into the kitchen, turning away from her and busied myself with making the coffee.

'We . . . we were . . . I mean . . . we . . . we do.' I stammered and knew my face was scarlet. 'I . . . it's nothing, Gwen. Really.'

The spoon in my hand clattered against the cup and I hurriedly put it down and took a deep breath.

Gwen changed her tack. She sat down and called to me through the open door.

'Oh, well, that's alright then. But, as I said, we've missed you both. I do know how much you've had to do just lately with it being the end of term and everything but now that you're on holiday and have more time, are you coming over? Arthur is longing for a game of chess, I'm longing for some female company . . . and that little girl of yours . . . and perhaps you could give Major some exercise . . . or Dolly.'

I smiled in spite of myself and, feeling a little more in command, joined Gwen in the sitting room and put down the tray of coffee and biscuits with studied care. I pushed my hair off my forehead and looked down into her kindly face to give her my best smile.

'Why, of course we'll come over. How about Friday afternoon? Would that be a good time? I need to go into town on the market bus tomorrow to do some urgent shopping. I don't think I have a thing to eat in the house! I've arranged for Jenny to spend most of the day with Dora.'

Gwen looked at me with bright and perceptive eyes but if she saw beyond the smile I had pinned to my face, she gave no sign but merely nodded and said that Friday would be fine. Almost too casually, she added,

'Unless you've made other plans, why not come over in the morning and stay for lunch? I'm afraid you won't see Andrew, though. He will be away for the weekend at a conference.'

I felt the tension ease from my shoulders and readily agreed as Jenny came skipping in, delighted to see her 'Aunty Gwen' and to regale her with the latest exploits of Tabitha. The next half hour passed easily and enjoyably.

When Gwen had gone and I was busy in the kitchen, I took myself to task . . . yet again. I mustn't make mountains out of molehills, I told myself resolutely. Life has just got to go on as before or I shall spoil things for Jenny . . . and myself. We have the chance to be happy and settled here and already I have such very good friends. I just got things wrong with Andrew, that's all and I shall somehow have to convince him that I only intend to be a friend . . . or even just an . . . an aquaintance.

A fleeting thought of his kiss swirled through my mind and I caught my breath on a sigh and banged the rolling pin in my hands down on to the pastry I was making. Which did it no good at all.

'It's a good day for the market,' remarked a beaming Dora, as Jenny was delivered to her the next morning. 'You know what they say, it allus rains on a Thursday . . . but it ent today.'

We both looked up into a cloudless blue sky and I agreed that it was certainly a glorious day but I wasn't allowed to enthuse about the weather any further.

'That old bus is a-coming, my woman.' Dora was peering down the village street. 'You'd best look sharp,' and I was waved off in a hurry.

I returned, laden and after unpacking my bags and stowing everything away, made myself a quick cup of coffee before whistling Jess up for her walk. Usually Jenny and I took her together but this morning I felt like walking briskly and Dora had told me to take my time over fetching Jenny home. I looked at my watch and realised that in all probability Jenny would be tucking into some lunch anyway.

'Come on, girl.' I bent down and fondled the eager dog's ears. 'We'll stretch our legs, shall we?'

Feathery tail waving joyously, Jess danced in front of me, tugging at the lead.

'You can come off your lead when we get to the bridle path,' I promised her and we set off, both of us enjoying a faster pace than usual. For Jenny's chubby little legs usually set our pace and there was often a lot of dawdling.

We soon reached the bridle path which led away from the road, through a couple of rough grazing fields and into the woods. I knew this way well for it was one which I had often used when exercising Dolly. Once I had made sure there were no cattle in the fields this day I bent down and released the impatient dog who tore off ahead of me.

I tramped energetically along, enjoying the warmth of the sun on my bare arms and the feel of the gentle summer breeze lifting tendrils of my hair. I felt at peace with the world, happy and relaxed and I suppose it showed in the way I walked and swung the lead in my hand.

Andrew must have seen me before I noticed him ride out of the dappled shade of the woods into the sunshine. I shaded my eyes from the glare and waited for him to come up to me, my heart hammering in the most absurd way. Perhaps now we could talk to each other and sort out just what had gone wrong.

He neither looked at peace nor relaxed. His face looked cold and set and I was reminded irresistibly of our very first meeting.

I wondered for a moment if he intended to ride straight past me so I held up my hand and called his name.

'Andrew . . . Andrew, stop for a minute,' I said, breathlessly. 'We . . . we need to talk.'

He reined in his horse and looked

down at me morosely but I saw this as an opportunity to put things right between us and, summoning up courage from somewhere, smiled tentatively up at him.

'I've been wanting to speak to you.'

'Indeed,' he gritted. 'I can't imagine why.'

I could feel my legs begin to tremble and I laid an uncertain hand on Major's shoulder. The big horse quivered and tossed his head as if he could sense my inner distress.

'Please, Andrew. There are . . . some things we . . . we need to sort out.'

He swung his leg over the saddle and dropped effortlessly down.

'Well?' he said, distantly.

'About that day at the show . . . ' I took a deep and steadying breath and smiled up at him, trying to be as casual as possible, afraid of embarrassing him.

'I'm sorry that we missed each other but I suppose it was just one of those things. It didn't matter you know.' I continued, in what I thought was a perfectly innocent attempt to smooth things over. 'We were perfectly alright. We had a lovely time.'

He glowered down at me even more and Ruth's words about waifs and strays pricked my memory and my chin went up of its own accord. He needn't look at me like that, I thought. I didn't let *him* down.

I felt the first stirrings of anger and my smile slipped. Throwing all caution . . . and tact . . . to the winds, I let fly.

'I don't need picking up and rescuing like a stray dog, you know. I'm quite capable of living my own life and . . . and finding my own entertainment.'

Even as the words left my mouth I felt horrified at what I was saying.

He flung the reins down savagely and Major shied and backed away but was unheeded.

Reaching out, he gripped my shoulders with bruising fingers and my head jolted back.

'I'll bet you are,' he ground out. 'I'd believe you to be capable of anything.

You pretty little bitches are all alike.'

I stared at him in shocked disbelief and although anger blazed from his white face somehow I knew there was pain and hurt behind it.

'Andrew, no . . . no . . . ' I half sobbed, but he ignored me.

'You wind a man up until he doesn't know where or what he is and then go off with someone new and I suppose you try the same tricks on them. Perhaps you went a bit further with Bill Thompson than you did with me, eh? Did he have more to offer?' And he shook me so roughly that my head snapped back and forth.

'Andrew . . . please . . . please listen. It wasn't like that at all.' I could feel the blood draining from my face. This was a nightmare.

Before I could say another word, his hands slid down from my shoulders and he pulled me savagely towards him. Bending his head his mouth came down on mine with punishing swiftness and, fiercely and cruelly, his lips and tongue took their toll. There was no way of stopping him and I'm very much afraid that most of me didn't want to anyway. His kiss became more searching and passionate and his hands meanwhile roved and caressed me, holding me closer and ever closer until, my senses swimming, I began to feel that we were almost becoming fused into one being. I was no longer in control and my whole self reacted instinctively. My arms went up around his neck, my hands entwined themselves in his dark hair and I arched against him, the dark tide of desire rising with every heartbeat in spite of myself. Some small part of my mind was despairingly telling me that this was all wrong . . . there was a bad feeling about it . . . but the rest of my mind and body swamped all sensible thoughts in a rising flood of passion.

It was Andrew who broke free first. He pushed me away with such force that I staggered and would have fallen if I hadn't come up against Major's shoulders. I leaned against the big horse for support, my hand going up to my bruised and trembling mouth and stared at this man who somehow almost seemed a stranger. My mind was racing but not a word would come and I felt shivery and sick.

'For all your pretty face and beguiling ways, you're not to be trusted.'

His voice was low and full of pain . . . and broke my heart.

'I could take you right now if I wanted to. Don't deny it.'

With one lithe bound he was back in the saddle and scowled down at me grimly.

'Well, don't worry. I don't want you. Anyone else can have you. I went through all this once before. I should have known and had more sense. When I first saw you, you reminded me of Margaret. I was right. You're just as self-seeking and two-faced. But, God help me . . . I thought . . . '

He whirled Major round and I stumbled back as the horse, already jittery, leapt forward. Regaining my balance, I stared after him as he rode hell-for-leather across the fields, stupid tears spurting from my eyes and pouring down my cheeks.

'How could you?' I whispered out loud. 'Oh, how could you?'

As they disappeared towards the roadway my shaking knees just refused to hold me up a moment longer and I sank down on to the rough grass and hid my face in my hands. I'm ashamed to say that I just gave way to all the tumultuous emotions that had plagued me over the last few weeks and wept bitter tears.

'I hate you, Andrew Bruce,' I muttered. 'I hate you.' But I knew I lied.

Returning from her foray in the woods, Jess bounded up to me and then stopped short. She whined softly and pushed a cold nose against my hands, then sat down at the side of me, quivering in the way dogs have when they know something is very wrong. It was the warmth of that small body leaning up against me that penetrated my misery and I lifted my head and blinked furiously.

I reached out and hugged her, sniffing away my tears and gaining some small measure of comfort from the contact.

'Oh, Jess. What am I to do? It's all such a mess.'

She whined and wriggled free. As far as she was concerned, the sound of my voice had put matters back to normal and it was time to go on with the walk. She ran along the path, then stopped and turned and barked, tail wagging joyfully.

'Yes, I'm coming,' I said and got tiredly to my feet and searched for a hanky. I blew my nose and scrubbed at my eyes feeling as if I had just come through a hurricane.

On my way back to the villlage I resolutely made up my mind to keep as far away from Andrew Bruce as I possibly could. My desolation turned to anger as his words repeated themselves in my mind. How dare he say such things, I thought. How dare he! He never even gave me a chance to speak.

Whatever was all that about, anyway? Why should he have been so angry with me? If he is about to get engaged to Ruth it shouldn't have mattered to him at all that I had apparently preferred Bill. Not that I did. Surely no-one would get so steamed up just because of hurt pride?

Over and over again I recalled the events of the past few weeks and could come to no conclusion. I just can't think about it any more, I told myself wearily. I'm too muddled to think straight. I felt tears well up again but, horrified at myself, choked them back fiercely and strode on with a subdued Jess on her lead, into the village and down the street to fetch Jenny home.

8

The next morning, while at breakfast, Jenny spooned more cornflakes into her mouth and remarked indistinctly, 'I'm going to have a ride on Old Moke today, aren't I, Mummy?'

She looked at me and, at my silence, asked anxiously, 'It is Friday today, isn't it? Auntie Gwen said Friday.'

'Yes love,' I reassured her. 'Yes, we're going over in a little while.'

But I don't want to, I thought. However, relying on Gwen's assurance that Andrew would have gone to his conference, I half-heartedly attended to a few household chores and then the two of us set off down the village street to Croxfield Hall. Jenny skipping along beside me, chattered away happily but I answered her absently, my mind very much elsewhere. Not that she seemed to mind or even notice. In her small world the sun was hot, long days of freedom stretched in front of her and today was going to be lovely. She relapsed into contented silence, obviously thinking of the treat in store.

As we turned in at the wrought iron gates I found myself looking anxiously up the driveway but there was no sign of Andrew's elderly estate car and I sighed thankfully. Gwen had obviously been watching out for us for she appeared at the doorway with a welcoming smile and Jenny ran the last few yards to greet her.

'Isn't it an absolutely gorgeous day? How's my girl, then?'

She picked Jenny up and gave her a hug, which was returned unhesitatingly. Putting her down, she took her hand and, as I reached them, linked her arm through mine.

'It's so nice to see you. I know it's only been a short while but we have missed you. Come along in.'

I was in a quandary. I was positive that Andrew would be opposed to me taking Major out and equally sure that very soon Gwen would be suggesting that I did so. How on earth am I going to get out of this, I worried to myself. With my mind on this problem, I hardly tasted the coffee that Gwen handed to me as we sat out in the garden.

I had underestimated Gwen's intuition and understanding. From what she had said the last time we met she was aware of something wrong between Andrew and myself. She had obviously given this some thought and been busy.

She put her cup down carefully,

'Oh, Emma, my dear, I hope you won't mind but this farmer friend of ours asked if we could keep his little mare over here during the school holidays and if you would take her out now and again. He is so busy with the harvesting just now and hasn't time for exercising her. You won't mind taking Dolly out instead of Major, will you?' . . . and she looked at me with those very perceptive blue eyes, her head tilted enquiringly.

'Oh no, Gwen. Not at all . . . and . . . and thank you.'

I'm sure she knew what I was really thanking her for and felt a rush of warmth and . . . yes . . . love . . . for this kindly understanding woman. So like my dear Aunt Maggie in many ways. Jenny danced up then to tug at her arm and the moment of emotion passed.

'Major had a good gallop yesterday,' continued Gwen, smoothly, 'So he will be quite content for the time being.' She gave me a quick glance but I looked away.

With Jenny bouncing up and down next to us, impatiently waiting for her ride on the donkey, there was neither time nor place for further conversation, sad or otherwise, so we laughingly allowed ourselves to be hurried off.

I promised Arthur that we would have a game of chess after lunch.

'And I'll beat you this time!' I called over my shoulder as Jenny tugged on my hand.

As I saddled Dolly I lifted my face to the warm soft breeze.

'It's going to be a beautiful day, Gwen.'

'Mmm, yes.' Gwen heaved Jenny on to Old Moke's back and the patient animal turned his shaggy head and nudged her, waiting for his usual carrot.

'My word, Jenny. You are growing into a big girl. You must weigh a ton!'

Jenny giggled happily and Gwen continued, 'Where are you going to ride, Emma?'

'I think I'll go a different way to the one I usually go. I'll go over the river and through the woods there. Then I'll come out by Swinton and . . . oh, blow.'

Gwen turned her head enquiringly and I tossed down my riding hat with a certain amount of exasperation.

'The strap's broken. Oh, well, I'll manage without it for once.'

Gwen shook her head and looked doubtful.

'Borrow Andrew's,' she said.

My refusal was a shade too vehement

and she gave me a startled look so I made myself laugh and say that it would probably be too big and any way, I was only going to amble along.

'It will be too hot to do anything else,' I added. 'Don't worry, Gwen, I shall be perfectly O.K.,' and I swung myself into the saddle, waved my crop at them gaily and trotted off down the drive.

As we turned into the water meadows I let Dolly have her head for a minute or two and we cantered briskly along towards the river. The wind lifted my hair and felt wonderful and my spirits began to lift with it. I slowed Dolly down then and we ambled as I had promised until we reached the river banks where both sides sloped down to a crossing place and there we contentedly splashed through the shallow water. The woods on the far side looked cool and inviting and we soon reached the bridle path that wound its way between the trees and bracken. A cock pheasant in all the glory of its magnificent plumage exploded almost from under Dolly's hoofs but she just tossed her head and never faltered. She was a most placid creature, which is why . . . in that dreadful time which still lay ahead of me . . . I had found her subsequent behaviour so difficult to understand.

She had quite plainly decided that it was too hot for any further great exertion and plodded along. I was quite happy with this and just enjoyed the scents and feel of the woodland. Butterflies flitted in and out of the sunshine where it penetrated through the trees and dappled the pathway ahead and wood pigeons murmured drowsily. I caught a glimpse of a grey squirrel in one of the taller trees and then caught sight of an alien figure. I reined Dolly in and, shading my eyes, peered over the undergrowth but whoever it was had disappeared. But my interest was aroused and, after turning the next corner, I stopped and scrutinised the woodland again. This time I got a good view of a furtive figure in a scruffy old green jacket hurrying away between the trees. I shook my head and pulled a face for I had recognised that shifty character. It was Albert Pegg, young George's ne'er-do-well father and if my guess was correct he was busy with a quiet bit of poaching. He wouldn't be in these woods just for a walk. These woods belonged to the Thompsons and he would be in dire trouble if caught. Bill had once told me what a thorn in his father's side Albert Pegg was and how he had been threatened with prosecution more than once. Still, it was nothing to do with me so I shrugged my shoulders and carried on.

The sun beat down and I lifted one hand off the reins to push my hair from my forehead. I remember thinking that I really must go into town and get it trimmed and as I sat back in the saddle, following the meandering path, completely relaxed, in no way was I prepared for the disaster which erupted from the next turning. I still don't remember all the details even after all the time which has gone by since that dreadful day.

There was a pounding of hoofs and a frantic scream and the sun was abruptly blotted out by a huge rearing blackness. I saw wild eyes and a flaring mane and a foam-flecked mouth baring wicked teeth. This could only have been in the split second before there was a terrible blow to my shoulder and I felt myself flying through the air ... and the ground came up to meet me. I remember hearing Dolly squeal and was filled with a dreadful, searing pain until, mercifully, a different kind of blackness enveloped me and I was whirled away into oblivion.

... I seemed to be surrounded by a grey swirling fog. I wanted to call out for help but although I opened my mouth and tried my best I could make no sound at all. What had happened? ... Where was I? There were blurred glimpses of a dark kind of blue and nebulous faces swam into view and then dissolved like wraiths . . . Aunt Maggie? . . . I called for her but another face seemed to float above me and I struggled to reach out.

Wicked pain shot through my head and body and my world disintegrated into blackness again . . .

. . . I cautiously opened my eyes and although the walls that I could see around me wavered slightly at first, eventually they ceased their dance and became firm and reassuring. I was in bed and, from the feel of things, well and truly trussed up. I turned my head . . . extremely slowly and carefully . . . and made out a familiar figure at the bedside.

As I blinked and focussed my gaze, I heard Gwen's voice calling urgently to someone. She bent down to lay her cheek gently against mine and then stood up and scrabbled in her bag for a tissue and dabbed at her eyes as the nurse came bustling up.

'Oh, Emma, my poor love. I am so

glad you're back with us.'

A rosy-cheeked young woman in the dark blue uniform of a ward sister bent over me.

'Well, that's better. I'll go and let the doctor know that she's come round, Mrs. Bruce. Don't try to move, Emma. Are you fairly comfortable?'

I rolled my eyes at her and she took that for a 'yes' and hurried off. Comfortable I was not but at least that dreadful pain was gone. Although I had a nasty feeling that it was only hovering in the background waiting to pounce. With an effort I turned my head towards Gwen and asked the most obvious of questions. My voice came out like a thread, whispery and with no strength at all.

'What happened, Gwen?'

She smiled reassuringly and reached for my hand and I gripped her fingers thankfully.

'Dolly threw you for . . . for . . . for some reason. We were getting just a little bit worried for you'd been gone a long time and then Dolly came trotting up the drive on her own. We were really worried then and called up everyone we could to search for you. The police found you . . . and . . . and . . . on the . . . the bridle path in Thompson's wood.'

'Jenny?' I whispered.

'Oh, Jenny's fine,' she answered swiftly. 'She's with me until we get you right again. She's with Dora at the moment and Dora will be looking after Jess and Tabitha so you are not to worry about anything at all. Just rest and get better.'

I managed another word. 'Dolly?'

'Yes, she's . . . she's fine.'

There seemed to be something evasive about her tone and I wondered muzzily just how badly I was hurt. I couldn't seem to feel my left arm at all and I knew my head was bandaged from when I had turned it slightly.

'Gwen . . . ' my voice was gaining a little strength . . . and even a touch of panic . . . but she seemed to know, instinctively, what was going through my muddled mind and gave my hand a little shake.

'Now, you're going to be fine. You had a nasty fall and you've broken your arm and must have hit your head on something really hard for you've been concussed. I'm sure you'll have bruises all over the place but after you've had a good rest you'll be as good as new.'

I could easily have imagined it was my Aunt Maggie talking . . . as if I were a child again and was being rallied after a fall and a cut knee! I smiled hazily, hardly noticing the nurse appearing at my bedside or the pin-prick in my arm and felt myself drift comfortably away.

How long I slept I don't know but the room was dark next time I opened my eyes. I must have moved or called out for there was a soft patter of feet and a nurse was at my side at once. My head ached and I felt disorientated . . . and had a raging thirst. I was made comfortable and must have been given another sedative because, although questions were running through my mind now, I couldn't concentrate on them. I tried to reach out to that ride and images of my last conscious moments.

What terror had come upon us so suddenly that peaceful summer morning? For somehow I knew there had been terror. What had made docile little Dolly throw me? I sank into a tormented and troubled sleep.

Gwen arrived early the next day, clutching a huge bunch of flowers. She put her head on one side and looked me over.

'I do think you've got a bit more colour today.' She turned to the ward sister who had come up behind her. 'She does look a bit better, doesn't she?'

Sister smiled and nodded.

'There doesn't seem to be any dreadful damage after all. The X-rays were quite encouraging. But we'll have to see what our specialist has to say. He'll be coming round this morning.'

She looked down at me.

'Is there anyone you would like him to speak to, Emma? Any family?'

I looked up at Gwen and then blinked and turned my face away.

'No Sister, thank you. I haven't got anyone. There's only me . . . and Jenny.'

'Jenny?'

'Emma's little girl. She's staying with me,' explained Gwen. Then she reached down and took my hand in her warm clasp. 'Emma's mistaken. She has got someone. She's got me . . . and my husband, Arthur. She might not realise it but she feels like one of the family as far as we're concerned.'

Sister nodded in a satisfied kind of way.

'Then I'll leave the two of you alone for now,' and she whisked away.

'Oh, Gwen. That's one of the nicest things anyone has ever said to me.'

I felt all weepy and choked. I wondered if she would feel the same way once she knew of the devastating rift between her beloved son and myself. In some inexplicable way she was almost attuned to my thoughts for, after undoing her coat and settling herself on the chair at the side of the bed, she continued calmly,

'We must get one or two things straight, my dear. First of all, I have a very strong suspicion that all is not well between you and that stiff-necked son of mine.'

My eyes flew wide open at that and she chuckled.

'Oh, yes. I love Andrew dearly but I'm not blind to his faults. In common with most mothers, I don't think he has many but I do know that he can make mistakes and doesn't always stop to find out why. That's in his private life. He is absolutely meticulous when it comes to dealing with a sick animal so why he can't be the same when dealing with people, I just don't know. However . . . whatever has gone wrong between the two of you is none of my business and I'm sure it will be resolved soon.'

'What I want you to be quite, quite

sure of, Emma, is that Arthur and I have grown very fond of you and your Jenny in your own right. I always wanted a daughter but the good Lord never saw fit to answer my prayers. You and Jenny are beginning to fill a gap in our lives that we would never admit to ourselves. Will you let us be, at least, your very loving friends?'

'Oh, but you are, Gwen. I can't think of anything I would like more.'

I cried and sniffed and blinked and scrubbed at my eyes with the tissue she pushed into my hand.

'Right,' she said briskly. 'Now we know where we are.'

'I know where I am right now,' I said gruffly, trying to hide the rush of emotion I had felt at Gwen's words. 'In a hospital bed without the remotest idea of how I got here.'

I expected at least a chuckle from her but she looked at me sombrely.

'Emma, can't you remember anything that happened? What made Dolly throw you . . . and with such force? Do try and remember. It's . . . it's really important.'

'I painfully turned my head and caught a very worried look on her face for a moment.'

'Why?' I asked, but she bit her lip and shook her head. I didn't pay too much attention at the time but concentrated instead on trying to recall my accident.

'It was such a lovely day,' I began, 'and Dolly and I were just ambling along enjoying the woodland. Honestly, Gwen if she'd been going any slower she'd have been going backwards! I can't understand how I came out of the saddle with such force. If she'd stumbled or something I wouldn't have fallen anyway. I'm sure I can keep my seat better than that.'

'Perhaps something jumped out in front of her,' said Gwen, slowly, 'and startled her. Did she rear at all?'

There was a strange intensity in her voice and I glanced at her, puzzled.

'Not that I can remember. The last

thing I can remember is the butterfly.'

'Butterfly?'

'Mmm. Yes. The woodland clearings seemed full of them and I remember watching a gorgeous Peacock butterfly that came so close that I thought it was going to settle between Dolly's ears. Funny, that seems so clear and . . . and then . . . Oh, Gwen, I can only remember a sort of jumble and noise and a feeling of absolute fright. What happened? . . . Why did . . .' and to my utter dismay, I began to feel tears slide down my face. My head hurt and I began to feel sick and dizzy. My one good hand reached out, flailing the air but Gwen caught it and spoke soothingly.

'Hush, dear. Don't try and remember any more. It will come back eventually. After all you've been lying there in a coma all this time. I shouldn't have asked you. It's too soon.'

'What do you mean, 'all this time'? How long have I been here?'

Gwen bit her lip. 'Now don't upset

yourself, Emma love. I suppose I'd better tell you. You've been unconscious for three days. We've all been very worried about you.'

She patted my hand. 'But not any more, remember. You are on the road to recovery now and we'll soon have you back home.'

'Oh, my poor Jenny. Whatever must she have been thinking?'

'We didn't tell her the details. Just that you had fallen off Dolly and hurt your arm and gone to hospital to have it made better. Of course she was upset at first but we've kept her cheerful.'

'Thank you Gwen. You have been good.'

I tried to lift myself up and then fell back with a groan I couldn't check. The wall on the other side of the ward began to bend and sway in a most peculiar manner so I shut my eyes to it and clenched my teeth to hold back the cry of total confusion and pain that was rocketing through me. I heard Gwen call out and someone came and I felt cool fingers on my wrist. I kept my eyes closed, fearing to see a world that was no longer safe but allowed solid walls to lurch and disintegrate.

'It's my fault. I shouldn't have tried to get her to remember the accident.' Gwen's voice was strained. 'Are they still out there? Don't let them come and bother her yet, will you?'

'No, I won't. Don't worry, she's not fit to be questioned yet. That's plain to see. Will you stay with her? I'll go and chivvy them off.'

The waves of pain and sickness were receding a little. 'Them?' I thought hazily, who does she mean?

I could hear Sister's voice from a distance and then a deeper voice answering her . . . a man's voice. Gwen must have joined them for I could hear her but she sounded far away. 'Please leave it to me,' I heard her say. 'I'll tell her as soon as it's safe to do so. It will be easier for her . . . '

I never heard the rest of her sentence, for, even as I wondered muzzily what would be easier, I felt myself plunging down into a blackness. It was the blackness of a nightmare and strange figures and images leapt out of nowhere and then swirled away. Weird black strands were tangling round me strangling and choking and as I pushed them away I found my hands full of a horse's mane. The horse was huge, out of all proportion and as I held on to its mane desperately, it tossed its head and flung me into the air, reaching out for me with wicked foam flecked teeth. The sound of hooves pounded in my head although it was more of a sensation than a sound. In a weird kind of a way I couldn't hear them and yet knew they were there, coming nearer and nearer. A white face swam into my vision and then was obscured by swirling mist and a blessed oblivion . . .

. . . I opened my eyes cautiously and was relieved to see that the walls were once more looking firm and solid. Gwen was still sitting by my bedside and she reached out and took my hand.

'Feeling a bit better?' she asked and I answered her with a smile.

'Strangely enough, Gwen, I actually do.'

It was true, I did feel stronger.

'Well, you've had a nice long sleep. A natural sleep this time. No sedatives. It will have done you the world of good and you can have a cup of tea in a minute. The tea-lady is just about due.'

That sounded like heaven.

As I gingerly sipped my tea through a most peculiar cup with a spout . . . for I still wasn't sitting up properly . . . I looked up at Gwen and said, hesitantly,

'I seem to remember something about my accident now. Was someone else there? With another horse?' and I told her of the fleeting memories that my nightmare had conjured up.

She looked at me with a very sorrowful look on her face and shook her head. For a moment she said nothing but gazed across the room, twisting her scarf in her hands until I thought she would surely tear it into shreds.

'What is it?' I asked. 'Tell me Gwen.'

'I wish with all my heart that I didn't have to,' she said and a chill went through me at her tone.

'Emma, love, you've got to know this and we . . . I . . . can't put it off any longer.' She turned towards my bed, took my cup away from me and reached out to hold my hands tightly in hers. 'There has been a . . . a terrible tragedy. There was someone else involved in your accident but . . . but it wasn't anyone with a horse. You must have dreamt that, my love. When the police found you, lying unconscious in the woods, they found someone else lying near you. It . . . it was little Duncan and . . . oh, Emma, I'm so very sorry to have to tell you this . . . you of all people, for I know you cared about him . . . Oh, Emma, he was dead.'

I stared at her in absolute bewilderment.

'No, I breathed. 'No, Gwen. He

couldn't possibly be,' but she nodded sadly.

'I'm afraid it's true, Emma. It appears he was very badly kicked in the head and must have died instantly. The police think that possibly he ran out from the trees and startled Dolly who must have reared and thrown you at the same time.'

'Gwen, I would have seen him. I know I would.'

Then the full horror of what she had told me hit home and I shut my eyes in a kind of denial and felt a shudder rip through the whole of my body.

'Oh, Duncan. Oh, poor little boy,' and I wept bitter tears.

Gwen held me for a while and then mopped up my tears and told me that the police were waiting to ask for details although she . . . and Sister . . . had held them off for as long as they could.

'Just tell them everything you can remember.' she advised. 'It wasn't your fault. It was obviously an accident.'

I choked on another sob.

'I feel it was my fault,' I whispered. 'But I never saw a sign of him, Gwen . . . anywhere.'

'Then just tell them that. Keep your chin up, love.'

She stood up and looked across the room. Sister was in the doorway and she nodded and turned to speak to someone outside. Then she came swiftly across followed by two figures in uniform. One, a burly thickset man and the other, a slim pleasant looking policewoman.

'Ten minutes and no longer,' said Sister, crisply, drawing the curtains round my bed with a practised swish. 'I don't want my patient to have any setbacks.'

Gwen left me with a lingering, backward look and I stared up at the two of them with misery in my heart for that poor little handicapped boy that I had grown to love and who had been treated so unfairly in his death as well as his life.

9

The police were very kind and didn't press their questions too much. I hesitated about whether to tell them of my vague and terrified memories of another rider and, when I finally did, it all sounded so strange that they looked distinctly sceptical. As well they might. It was beginning to sound more and more unreal to me. They probably thought I was trying to avoid the responsibility of poor little Duncan's death. It really wasn't that. Somehow I couldn't rid myself of the conviction that more had happened that morning than was apparent.

After they had gone and Gwen also, I lay there going over and over things in my mind. Why on earth had little Duncan been in the woods on his own that day? The times that both Douglas Rawdon and I had warned his feckless young mother about the dangers of letting him wander. I thought unhappily that I had never ever dreamed that I would be the one to be a source of disaster to him.

I remembered how that cock pheasant had rocketed from under Dolly's hooves that fatal morning and she had never turned a hair. Another thing . . . she was used to children. She wouldn't have suddenly gone berserk at a child jumping out of the undergrowth. If that is what he had done. Surely I would have seen him anyway? Unless that bang on the head had robbed me of my memory. And yet . . . and yet . . . I seemed to remember other details.

My worried thoughts went round and round.

If only someone else had been there to see what really happened. I wished . . . and then another memory jerked me so that I almost cried out. There had been someone else in the woods that day. Albert Pegg.

Perhaps he had seen what happened. Perhaps he had seen young Duncan.

Another grimmer thought struck me. He certainly wouldn't want to admit to being in the woods. If he did know anything, would he own up to it? And if he did would it help me anyway?

Thinking of poor little Mrs. Pegg and George, not to mention the rest of her brood, did I really want to get him into trouble with the police? No, it would be better if I spoke to him first.

I needed to know the truth. If the accident was due to any carelessness on my part then of course I would accept the responsibility. But I needed desperately to know.

My heart ached for little Duncan and his poor mother. Supposing it had been Jenny? How would I have felt? I knew too well that I would have been devastated. Useless tears slid down my cheeks and I wept for them both. I moved restlessly in my bed, seeking a more comfortable position. Tomorrow, I thought, tomorrow I will ask Gwen what to do. Or Arthur. For she had told me that they would both come to visit and bring Jenny with them. On that consoling thought I drifted off to sleep. I seemed to be sleeping a lot but I supposed that was nature's way of healing.

I waited very impatiently the next day for my visitors to arrive. The specialist came to see me in the morning and, after what seemed to be a great deal of poking and prodding, gave me the encouraging news that I would be able to return home very soon.

'Your arm and shoulder took a beating, Mrs. Dane,' he said cheerfully, 'so you'll have to keep that plaster on your arm for quite a while. But there shouldn't be any problems with it. It was a clean break and your shoulder is only bruised. It's rather strange,' he added thoughtfully, 'But I could swear, by its appearance, that the worst bruise on your shoulder was caused by an iron-clad hoof. Your horse must have kicked you when you were on the ground but . . . I don't know . . . the angle seems all wrong. It's as if that hoof was aimed straight at you before you hit the ground. But of course that's impossible. I haven't had much experience with horse-induced injuries . . . much more with those caused by motorbikes,' and he smiled down at me and ruefully shook his head.

'Anyway,' he continued more briskly, 'The stitches on that nasty cut on your head can come out the day after tomorrow and then we'll decide about you going home.'

He nodded and strode off, followed by his attentive entourage of nurses and interns.

I watched him go abstractedly, my mind fastening on one thing only. A glimpse of that rearing blackness and wild tossing mane had edged its way into my thoughts and I shuddered. Had it been reality or just a nightmare?

There was a bustle in the ward then as our lunch was pushed in on a trolley and the cheery ladies in their bright orange overalls handed us our meals and a good deal of jollity to go with them. They were a tonic in themselves.

The tonic I needed more than anything was the sight of my Jenny and at last, that evening, the visitors began to arrive. I saw Arthur first as Gwen pushed him ahead of her in his wheelchair and for a moment Jenny hung back, the poor lamb, overcome by the hospital atmosphere I suppose. Then she came at me in a rush and I hugged her as best I could with only one good arm. How wonderful it felt to have her little face snuggled into my neck in spite of the sharp twinges it caused. I endured them willingly.

Gwen came to my rescue and, once she had settled Arthur at my bedside, laughingly lifted Jenny off me and sat down with her on her knee.

'Sweetheart, your Mummy has a poorly arm. Be careful.'

Jenny reached out hesitantly and gently stroked my plaster.

'Does it hurt a lot, Mummy?' Her

eyes were wide and solemn.

'Not now, darling,' I reassured her, 'And the doctor says I can come home soon. Are you being a good girl for your Auntie Gwen?'

She nodded vigorously and Gwen kissed her cheek and answered for her.

'She's being as good as gold. Tell Mummy what you've been doing these last few days, pet.'

And I was given a blow by blow account of all her activities.

At last she ran out of steam and I seized my opportunity.

'Gwen,' and I gave her a speaking look. 'Would you be an angel and take Jenny to get a drink from the machine outside?'

She looked quizzically from me to Arthur and nodded.

'Of course. Come on, Jenny. You can put the money in the slot.' She looked over her shoulder as they went and grinned. 'I shall demand to hear all about it afterwards.'

'Well,' said Arthur, 'What's the secret then?'

'Oh, no secret, Arthur. I just wanted to ask you something and I didn't want Jenny taking it all in,' and I told him about Albert Pegg being in the woods that day.

It all came tumbling out, incoherently at first, until Arthur made me stop and gather myself together. As I told him of the vague memories of another rider and the specialist's comments about my bruising, he grew more and more thoughtful. I lay back on my pillows, exhausted and he sat quietly for a moment.

Stealing a look at him, I said miserably. 'You think I'm snatching at straws, don't you? Trying to avoid the responsibility for little Duncan's death. Honestly, it isn't like that, Arthur. I just want to know the truth. I'm beginning to feel I'm going mad. I . . . '

He held up his hand.

'No . . . no, Emma. I don't think that for one moment. I do understand. I'll go and see Albert and find out if he saw anything. Don't worry, he'll talk to me. I know one or two things about that rascal. I really think you'll have to tell the police though, that you saw him that morning.'

'He'll get into trouble and what about that poor wife of his and . . . and George . . . and the other children?'

'They'll survive it. Anyway, I'll see what he has to say first.'

He sat as if lost in thought for another moment and then stirred and sat up straight as if he had come to a decision.

'I wasn't going to tell you this just yet but now I think I'd better. I was puzzled about the state of Dolly when she came home without you. I knew you wouldn't have ridden her hard but she was in a real lather and very jittery. She was really spooked and it took Gwen all her time to catch her. I couldn't understand it at all. Another thing. She had a nasty gash across her shoulder and the young chap who is standing in for Andrew had to put a couple of stitches in. Neither of us could understand how she had got it. It didn't look like the kind of injury she would have got by running off through the trees.'

He stopped for a moment and shook his head in a baffled kind of way.

'She had quite a weal on her hindquarters. The sort of thing that's caused by a crop coming down too fiercely.'

He looked at me intently then, with those keen dark eyes of his.

'Now I am positive that you wouldn't do a thing like that unless there was a very imperative reason?' There was a hint of a question in his voice.

I shook my head.

'No, Arthur, I wouldn't and there was no reason. Dolly and I were just dawdling along without a care in the world.' Not that such a statement was strictly true but the cares I had buried were not the kind that would have caused me to ill-treat Dolly, even if I had allowed them to surface.

Gwen and Jenny came back into the ward then so he leaned forward and patted my hand.

'Don't worry about it, my dear. Dolly's fine now and I'll deal with that other matter as soon as I can.'

He turned to Jenny and pointed a finger.

'You've been at the raspberryade again,' he said sternly and she giggled happily.

'Have I got a red mouth, Mummy? Uncle Arthur teases me when I have a drink,' and the tension lifted and the rest of the evening passed enjoyably.

Most of Arthur's remarks had puzzled me but one in particular stuck in my mind. Who was this young man who had attended to Dolly? Why not Andrew? I wondered also what Andrew would be thinking about this whole sorry business. Another nail in my coffin, I thought bitterly.

I just couldn't bring myself to ask what I wanted to know.

It was Jenny who innocently brought the subject up.

'Oh, Mummy, there's another big

dog with his leg all bandaged up. Mr. Dawlish had to sew it.' Her voice was suitably horrified.

'Mr. Dawlish?' I queried lightly.

'Oh, yes,' answered Gwen. 'I told you that Andrew had gone north to a conference, didn't I?'

I nodded and she continued. 'Well, apparently he met some colleagues up there that he hadn't seen for ages and they persuaded him to join them for a walking holiday for a couple of weeks. He decided it all on the spur of the moment, arranged for this young man to act as his locum and off he went.'

I could hear a tinge of worry in her voice as she added, 'It's not like him to act so impulsively. I never even got a chance to speak to him because he rang and left all the details on our answering machine while we were out.'

She looked at me pensively. 'He doesn't know anything about the accident yet, Emma and I can't tell him because goodness knows where he is right now. He didn't leave any telephone number.'

'Now don't worry about it.' Arthur leaned forward and, taking hold of her hand, gave it a little shake. 'He'll only be gone for two weeks. It's time he had a break anyway. By the time he comes home Emma will have nearly recovered and we shall have everything sorted out.'

'What do you mean, sorted out?' Gwen looked at him doubtfully.

'Tell you later.'

I stirred restlessly. 'If you get to speak to him on the phone, don't bother him with all this.'

'But he'll want to know,' said Gwen, puzzled.

I just couldn't help it. I must have been in a weakened state or I would have had better control over my feelings.

'No, Gwen, he won't want to know.' I almost snapped. Instantly I was horrified at myself. 'Oh, Gwen, I'm sorry . . . I . . . I don't know what's the

285

matter with me. But please don't tell him.'

'It's alright, my dear. I won't just yet but he'll have to know some time. I don't suppose I shall get a chance to speak to him anyway for we really don't know where he is at the moment. He could be tramping all over the Pennines for all we know.'

She spoke soothingly and I hid my confusion in Jenny's curls, thankful that she was cuddled up to me.

Looking through the wide window I could see that the blue sky was deepening into dusk. It was time for them to go. How I longed to be going with them.

Another visitor arrived the next day. A visitor who pushed her way through the usual throng with unheeding intensity.

She looked wildly about her, frantic eyes searching every bed until they lit on mine.

Duncan's mother.

She gripped the rail at the bottom of

my bed and stared at me with a face full of pain and hatred.

'It's a pity you hen't got more damage done to you. It's a pity you weren't killed too,' she cried, her voice rising hysterically.

I shrank back against the pillows but the relentless voice went on.

'My pore little lad never had much chance. It weren't fair, the way he wus but he never did no harm to no-one.' She gulped and dashed a hand across her eyes and her voice rose almost to a shriek.

'Now he's gone a 'cos of you. Murderer. Thass what you are. Murderer.'

The room whirled around me and I felt sick. I tried to reach out a hand to her.

'Mary . . . Oh, Mary . . . I'm sorry . . . I'm so sorry . . . I never saw . . . he wasn't . . . '

She took no notice of my stumbling words but covered her face with her hands and wailed.

The other visitors were rooted to the spot ... in shock, I suppose ... but Sister must have heard the commotion for she came in at a run and took in the situation at once, for she was at Mary's side in a split second and gently urged the weeping overwrought young woman away to her office outside.

I wanted to cry out ... to scream out ... that I didn't deserve such a terrible accusation but I felt frozen. I closed my eyes and huddled in my bed. I heard the other visitors move at last to other bedsides and shocked whispers grow into the louder hum of normal conversation but I didn't dare to open my eyes. Never had I felt so unhappy and alone.

Sister came back after what could only have been a few minutes but felt like an eternity.

'Are you alright, Emma?' I felt her hand on mine and her voice was anxious.

I nodded but kept my eyes screwed

shut, fearing to see condemnation on her face too.

'I'm so sorry. I wish I'd seen her in time.'

The compassion in her voice was my undoing and I couldn't stop tears from sliding down my face. I turned my head and buried my face in the pillow.

'Look, your friend will be here soon. I'll pull the curtains round your bed for a bit.'

I whispered my thanks and she pulled the curtains and left me to a welcome privacy. By the time Gwen arrived I was able to greet her with some measure of composure but she was horrified to hear of what had happened.

'You're as white as a sheet, Emma. My poor girl. Oh, I wish I'd been able to prevent this.'

'She's right, Gwen. It seems that I . . . I was responsible for his death, so . . . yes . . . I . . . I killed him. Poor little Duncan. Oh, Gwen, I can't bear it. Poor Mary. If it had been my Jenny I would have felt the same. Oh, the poor, poor woman.'

She held me in her arms but I could find no solace anywhere and felt as if my heart would break.

I was kept in hospital for two more days and they seemed like for ever. Douglas and Elsie came to visit me and Douglas gave me a certain degree of comfort when he told me that he had heard of Mary's accusations and immediately gone to see her.

'I went round to help as soon as I heard of little Duncan's accident,' he said. 'She hasn't anyone in the village to sort things out for her. Of course she was devastated but I had no idea that she would come all this way to make trouble for you. When I heard what she had done, I went straight round to see her again.'

Elsie patted my shoulder. 'You really mustn't blame yourself, Emma. That poor little boy must have dashed straight out in front of you. It was a pure accident. The way that Mary let him roam round the countryside it's a wonder something hadn't happened to him before this,' and her voice sharpened.

Douglas shook his head. 'Now, Elsie don't be too hard on the girl. You know how feckless she is and given her circumstances and the life she's had up to now, it's understandable.'

Elsie looked across at her husband with loving exasperation.

'You'd find excuses for the devil himself.'

'I don't think you're right there,' he grinned at her then turned back to me, 'but she's right about one thing, Emma. You really mustn't blame yourself. Try to overlook what Mary said. She was overwrought and frantic and I'm sure she didn't mean those dreadful words.'

I remembered the distressing scene of the day before and Mary's white and anguished face and shivered. Douglas must have noticed for he gave me a searching look before he continued.

'I told her that none of us can be sure

of what exactly happened yet but that she could be sure that it was a complete accident. She knows that she should never have allowed him to stray so far away and has probably got feelings of guilt mixed up with her grief and, human nature being what it is, has looked for something or someone to hit out at. I also reminded her of how you really loved that little boy and did so much for him. We know how he improved while in your care. You wouldn't have hurt a hair on his head. She knows this deep down, Emma.'

'Thank you, Douglas.' I managed to summon up a smile. 'That was really kind of you.'

I felt tremendously touched . . . and marginally more cheerful and Elsie began to chat of other things and told us little stories of her hospital work to make us chuckle and pass the time.

But nothing could alter the fact that a child had lost his life . . . and I was involved.

Gathering my belongings together

finally, I looked round the ward and reflected on how my life had changed in the last few days. I wondered, with some trepidation, what lay ahead of me. The police had visited me again, merely to see if I had remembered anything further and to tell me that there would be an enquiry later on. I was dreading this. Arthur had advised me to say nothing yet about Albert Pegg.

'Give me a chance to speak to him first,' he had said. 'I did drive down to see him but he was out somewhere . . . up to no good, I don't doubt. He'll clam up if the police question him.'

So, rightly or wrongly, I had kept my counsel for the time being.

As I zipped up my holdall, a nurse popped her head round the ward entrance and called to me.

'Your friends are here, Emma.'

I looked up, expecting to see Gwen as she had promised to collect me and wondering who else was with her.

There stood Peggy, grinning all over

her face, with Gwen behind her looking just as pleased.

'Oh, Pegs! Oh, how good to see you. Whatever are you doing here?' I cried as she hurried over to give me a careful hug.

Holding me at arm's length, she looked me up and down.

'Emma Dane, I can't leave you on your own for five minutes, can I,' she said with mock severity and seized my bag. 'Come on, let's get you home and you can tell me all about it.'

We said our goodbyes and thanks and made our way out of the hospital to Peggy's waiting car.

'I suppose this is your doing, Gwen?' and I squeezed her hand.

'Not entirely,' she answered cheerfully. 'Both Dora and I thought your friend ought to know of your accident and so I rang Peggy . . . I may call you Peggy? . . . the other day and she immediately suggested that she should come down and stay to look after you for a little while. We thought it an excellent idea. I had planned for Jenny and you to stay with us, you know, but maybe this is better?'

I must admit to being relieved in a way. I had realised that I would need help but the thought of being in Andrew's home posed problems.

'Oh, Gwen, you are kind. It was so good of you to offer to have us but I've got to learn to manage for myself . . . and you've done so much already.'

'Well, we're all going to have a meal together first and then Peggy will take you and Jenny home and you can talk everything over to your heart's content. Dora has done some shopping for you so there's plenty in the house.'

I turned to my friend who was concentrating on manoeuvring the car through Norwich's busy streets but listening to this as well.

'Pegs, I can't begin to tell you how good Gwen has been to Jenny and me. I don't know what I'd have done without her.'

Gwen shook her head at me, smiling.

'Oh, you'd have managed, my girl.'

'Maybe but you made it so much easier . . . ' A different thought had struck me. 'Pegs, weren't you supposed to be going to Italy for a holiday?'

'Yes, and I still am. I was lucky. The company I was going with had a last minute cancellation so they very kindly altered my dates and I shall now be going in two week's time.'

'Peggy! You might have lost your holiday because of me.' I shook my head at her and lapsed into silence, my thoughts turning to how lucky I was to have such true and staunch friends.

'You'd have done the same for me.' replied Peggy, lightly. 'Everything's O.K.' and there we let the matter rest and the journey home passed swiftly as Peggy brought me up-to-date with news of Norton Primary and mutual friends and aquaintances.

We arrived at Croxton Hall to be welcomed by Arthur and Dora with smiles all over their faces and by Jenny with a strangling hug which did wonders for my sore heart ... but absolutely nothing for my broken arm, which was now encased in a sling.

'Your meal's all ready for you, Mrs. Bruce.' Dora nodded her head and bustled off into the kitchen for a last minute check up and then into her coat and away with a few parting words for me.

'Now, don't you forget, my woman, anything you want doing, just say. Miss Mitchell, you be sure and let me have all the washing and I'll attend to it and the ironing.'

'With the greatest of pleasure, Mrs. Parfitt,' chuckled Peggy although I shook my head at them both.

'You'd better be careful. I could get to like all this pampering.'

Later that evening when Peggy, Jenny and I were back in the schoolhouse and Jenny had been tucked up in bed, I brought my friend up to date with all that had happened over the last few weeks. Well, almost all. I made light of the disastrous Norfolk Show Day although I did suddenly remember the crumpled bit of note that I has found by my gate and rooted about in the kitchen drawer until I found it. I showed it to her just to see what she would make of it rather than anything else. She studied it far more thoughtfully than I thought it deserved. I told her nothing of my later meeting with Andrew. That was something I couldn't bear to speak of.

We talked far into the night and it was a relief to tell her about the accident. Her blunt common sense helped me to get a lot of things into perspective. But, as ever, she wasn't without sensitivity and insight.

'I think there's more to all this than meets the eye,' she said at last, standing up and stretching. 'But let's go to bed now, Em. You should have been tucked up hours ago.'

I jumped up, full of compunction. 'So should you. You must be tired after that long drive down here. Tell you what, we'll have a lie-in in the morning.'

'Maybe . . . if Jenny and your animals will let us. But I tell you one thing, Em. I have a definite feeling that there is still a great deal to be found out. Something doesn't ring true about your accident . . . and there are other things. What if that man Pegg is more involved than we realise. Is he a violent man?'

We stared at each other in horror as various scenarios nudged their way into our minds.

'Anyway, I shan't rest until we know the truth about it all.'

'Sherlock Mitchell to the rescue!' I scoffed, but I was very touched and a tiny thread of hope made itself felt as I drifted off to sleep that night.

We had scarcely finished our breakfast the next morning when there was a light-hearted tattoo on the door. Peggy went to answer it and returned with a familiar figure behind her.

'A visitor for you, Em.' Her voice was amused.

'Hi, Emma. How are you?' and Bill Thompson breezed in with the biggest basket of fruit I have ever seen in my life and thrust it in my direction.

'Good heavens, Bill. Well, thank you, how lovely. I'm getting on fine thank you.'

I got up awkwardly from my chair.

'Peggy, this is Bill Thompson. He and his sister, Ruth, live in the next village. They are . . . are . . . Andrew's friends. I think I have told you of them? Bill, this is my good friend Peggy Mitchell who has come to stay for a few days.'

He gave me what could only be described as an old-fashioned look.

'Your friends too, Emma.'

They shook hands and Peggy tilted her head and grinned up at the tall figure which almost seemed to fill my tiny dining room.

'Oh yes, I'd heard about you.'

He looked down and gave her his most devastating smile.

'Nothing but good I hope?'

'Now, I shan't tell . . . and that will keep you on your toes,' and she smiled demurely.

Demurely? . . . Peggy?

'How about coffee?' I broke in before a mutual admiration society could begin to form. I could really do without Bill Thompson getting his feet under the table. 'Peggy, you'll have another cup, won't you?'

'Yes, O.K. But you sit down. I'll get it,' and she made for the kitchen.

Jenny had been eying the luscious basket of fruit so I gave her a handful of grapes, saying meanwhile, 'This was terribly extravagant of you, Bill. You really shouldn't have.'

'Think nothing of it. I would have come to the hospital to see you but they said you were soon coming home. I had to come and see how you were. Whatever really happened? Speculation is rife in the village.'

I didn't doubt that for a moment but was very reluctant to talk about it. However it seemed churlish not to tell him something so I just gave him the same bare details that I had given the police. Peggy came in then with the coffee and rescued me and our talk turned to general subjects and Jenny, bored with the grown-up conversation went off to play with Tabitha.

As he finally got up to go, he looked away from me and I sensed a certain embarrassment.

'Ruth . . . er . . . Ruth asked me to give you her good wishes. I think she will probably call in to see you.'

I rather suspected that was something he had dreamed up himself.

He looked at me then and his usually cheerful face looked uneasy.

'She hasn't been at all herself, just lately.'

I thought grimly that she ought to be feeling on top of the world with Andrew and I so alienated but I forced myself to ask,

'Why? What's the matter?'

He hesitated. 'I don't really know. She looks dreadful, hardly eats and stays up in her room all hours of the day. She's been like that for well over a week now and it's not like her at all.

Dad and I are beginning to get quite worried. Especially after what she did yesterday. That worried us more than ever.'

We both looked at him with concern.

'What happened?' I asked.

He ran his hand through his hair in an exasperated sort of way.

'She only went and cancelled her entry at next week's show-jumping event. She would have won it, hands down, I know. That stallion of hers is in top form. Although he won't be soon if she doesn't snap out of whatever's bothering her. She hasn't taken him out for well over a week and that's completely out of character for her. Especially when there's a jumping event looming ahead. He's eating his head off in idleness and I haven't time to exercise him.'

He laughed, ruefully.

'To be honest, even if I had, I think I'd fight shy of him. He's always been a wicked, hard to handle brute. Ruth is really the only one who can control him. Dad has always wanted her to sell him, afraid for her safety but she never would.'

'What's he like? To look at, I mean,' asked Peggy, casually. I glanced at her, surprised. Her voice had been almost too casual and I knew she didn't have the slightest interest in horses, anyway.

'Well, he's a magnificent animal actually. Coal black . . . and a black heart to match. Ruth named him Satan and it was a good choice. Just the opposite to my gentle mare. Remember her, Emma? And the colt? You should see him now.'

His voice warmed and a proud smile lit his face. 'Why don't you bring Jenny and your friend over to see him? Come to lunch or something.'

'Thank you, Bill. That would be lovely. But I don't know what our plans are just yet. We'll see.'

I ushered him out, making more non-committal noises and, thanking him again for his present, finally managed to shut the door on him.

I sat down and rested my head on my hands.

'I wonder how many more times I shall be asked to explain what happened?' and I couldn't help a tinge of exasperation creeping into my voice. 'I wish there was someone who could explain it all to me.'

Peggy shifted round in her chair and rested her arms on the table. She leaned forward urgently.

'Let's go and find that Albert Pegg. I know Arthur has tried to catch him but there's no reason why we shouldn't try as well. Or maybe his wife would know something. He may have talked to her.'

'I suppose we could. I've always got on well with Mrs. Pegg.' I stared into the dregs of my coffee cup and fingered the spoon absently. 'Did you hear what Bill said when he first came in? That speculation was rife in the village? I bet they've got me all tried, judged and convicted by now.'

'Then it's up to us to prove them wrong.' Peggy sat up straight and there was a distinctly martial flash in her eyes. 'Anyway, I've been doing a bit of speculating myself ever since that gorgeous hunk departed from your door.'

I looked up in amazement. 'What . . . oh, you mean Bill?' and I found myself giggling for the first time since this trouble had begun.

'Yes, I most certainly do.' Peggy spoke severely but couldn't keep an irrepressible grin from spreading across her face. 'What's the matter with you, girl? There are opportunities there.'

'Huh! But not for me, thank you. Oh, he's nice enough and good company but that's as far as it goes. What did you mean about speculating?'

'It's what he said about his sister and then, when he described her horse, it struck a chord . . . rang a bell . . . I don't know. I've just got a funny feeling about it all.'

'I know that horse,' I said slowly. 'He frightens me. I've seen Ruth ride him and he is magnificent but it takes her all her time to keep him in check. His eyes always look a bit wild. You get stallions like that sometimes that are unpredictable.'

Peggy leaned forward again. 'Emma . . .' and there was a disquieting note in her voice. 'If the last time Ruth took that horse out was over a week ago then . . .' and she hesitated and fiddled with the cup in front of her ' . . . then it's just possible that she could have been out on the same day as you.'

'Maybe so. What are you getting at, Pegs?'

She didn't answer me directly.

'Bill seemed to be worried about her.'

'Well, I can understand that. She's completely wrapped up in her horses usually. It just wouldn't be like her to neglect any of them.'

'I wonder what happened to make her do that? Something must have happened. Now you know I'm completely ignorant as far as horses are concerned, Em but tell me this. If she had taken a nasty toss would that account for it?'

I shook my head, decidedly.

'Oh no, not at all. For one thing, I doubt that she would have had a fall. She's an amazing horse-woman. And if by any chance she had, then it certainly wouldn't have put her off riding. No way.'

'Then it's got to be something worse. Something really bad. Like . . . like . . . ' and she reached across and gripped my hand. 'Em, could she have been in the same woods as you, that day?'

I looked across at her and felt a dawning horror.

'You don't think . . . ?' I breathed and then shook my head in disbelief.

Peggy finished my sentence for me.

' . . . that Ruth was involved in the accident too?'

'How could she possibly be? I would have known.'

'Don't forget that you collected an almighty bang on the head from somewhere which scrambled your brains for a bit. You've said that you couldn't remember everything. And supposing she came upon you suddenly and the horses collided or something . . . and . . . and . . . supposing little Duncan jumped out just at that moment? It would explain a lot.'

She jumped off her chair excitedly and paced up and down.

'Emma, that's got to be the answer. No wonder the wretched girl hides in her room and has turned against her horse. It was probably all her fault and she's letting you take the blame.'

I shook my head again.

'Surely not, Pegs. Why would she do that?'

'Oh, Em, wake up.'

She came round to me and gripped my shoulder, giving me a little shake.

'It seems to me that she wants you out of the way. I bet that affair of the Norfolk Show was all a put up job.'

All I could answer was 'Ouch!' and she let me go with a smothered exclamation.

'I'm so sorry, love. I was so carried away I forgot your bruises. Oh, I am sorry.'

'I'll live, don't worry. Pegs, isn't that just it? That you are getting carried away. This is all wild guesses. We are snatching at straws.'

'I don't think so. Come on, girl. Grab Jenny and we'll go for a ride,' and she strode out of the house, leaving me to call Jenny, put the dog in the kitchen, lock the door and follow behind at a run.

'Where are we going, Auntie Pegs?'

'Oh, just for a ride round, chick. It's a lovely day and we ought to be out in it,' was the airy reply.

But as Jenny scrambled into the back seat, Peggy asked me quietly, 'Which is the way to the Peggs' house?'

10

Mrs. Pegg was hanging her washing out on the line when we reached her gate and when she saw us she stuffed the clothes pegs into the pocket of her ragged cardigan, making it droop even further round her thin frame and hurried to meet us.

'Mrs. Dane, how are you? Eh, I was that sorry to hear of the accident. That pore little ol' boy . . . an' you with your arm in a sling. Eh, dearie me!'

But she looked at me without condemnation, only sympathy showing in her faded blue eyes.

'Is your husband in, Mrs. Pegg? I need to speak to him urgently.'

'Well, he should be around some-where,' and she turned around and yelled his name.

'Albert. Albert . . . yer wanted.'

Looking back at me over her shoulder,

she remarked, 'He's in demand. Old Mr. Bruce has been twice, trying ter catch 'im.'

Albert Pegg slouched round the corner of the house and his truculent expression grew grimmer when he saw me standing at his gate.

Ignoring me, he glared at his wife.

'Wotcher want?' he demanded.

The drab little woman bridled. 'Don't you be like that, Albert Pegg. Mrs. Dane wants a word with you. Come you up here.'

Turning back to me, she said hurriedly, 'Don't you mind him, my woman. He's a bit out 'o sorts this morning. Was it about our George, then? He 'ent been getting wrong?'

'No, no, Mrs. Pegg. Nothing like that. I just need your husband's help.'

She gave an expressive snort. 'Huh! That'll be a first,' but she kept her voice low and I heard Peggy, behind me, give an appreciative chuckle.

By this time Albert had reached us and, shoving his hands in his pockets, stood impassively, waiting.

'Mr. Pegg, I . . . were you . . . ' I was suddenly at a loss, wondering whether his wife knew of his illicit forays into Thompson's wood. Peggy had no such qualms however. She gave me a quick look and then squeezed my arm and stepped forward.

'What Mrs. Dane wants to know, Mr. Pegg, is whether you saw her in the woods that day of her accident.'

'Who says I wus in them woods?' he demanded.

'I saw you, Mr. Pegg,' I broke in. 'I saw you quite distinctly.' adding, as an afterthought, 'but I haven't mentioned it to anyone . . . yet.'

Mrs. Pegg glowered at him.

'You great fule. Wotcher want ter go into Thompson's woods for? You know what the old man said he'd do if you got caught in there once more. What'll we do if yer git sent down agin?'

'Hold yer row, woman.' He looked across at me and his shifty eyes glittered. 'Supposin' I wus there and supposin' I did see you, what do you want ter know for?'

'Mr. Pegg . . . please . . . did you see what happened? Did you see . . . Duncan . . . or . . . or anyone else?'

He shuffled his feet uneasily and then seemed to come to a decision.

'I en't sayin' I wus there. So I couldn't have seen nothin' could I?'

'Albert! Surely you can help Mrs. Dane? Just you think on of all she's done fer our George.'

He shook his head angrily. 'Leave orf, woman. I en't agoin' ter git mixed up in this an' thass a fact. I can't help her.'

With that, he turned on his heel and strode back up the path, the cinders flying from his boots.

She looked after him and shook her head dispiritedly.

'Eh, I'm sorry, Mrs, Dane.'

Realising that my one hope was on the point of disappearing fast, I brushed past her.

'Forgive me, Mrs. Pegg but I must

catch him,' and I flew down the path after him.

'Mr. Pegg, stop a minute,' and I reached out and grabbed his sleeve. It felt greasy under my fingers but I held on tight.

'Please, Mr. Pegg. Please tell me if you saw anyone else in the woods that day. I know you were there. Did you see Duncan? Did you see what happened?' My voice became choked. 'It's really so important to me,' and I tightened my grip on his sleeve even more, my hand trembling uncontrollably.

He turned and looked down at me with anger and I was afraid I had lost. Then a different expression chased across his features and he gave a sigh.

'Now look you here, Mrs. Dane, that little ol' mawther is dead and gone and nothin' can't bring him back. Everyone knows it must ha' bin an accident. It might jest as well ha' bin you what wus killed. You en't a-goin' ter git wrong fer it. Let it drop. Wotcher want ter go on at me for?'

I let go of him and said quietly, 'Because I have to know the truth, Mr. Pegg, and I have a feeling that you can tell me.'

He gave me a twisted smile that had no mirth in it whatsoever.

'Truth, is it? Well, I reckon I owe you that much . . . on account of our George.' Rubbing a grimy hand over his face, he gave me a sideways look.

'I en't bin much of a Pa to him and that's a truth. My missus is allus on about what you done fer him, so I'll tell you this. Yes, I did see that little ol' boy that day. It wus jest afore I saw you ploddin' along on Harrison's mare.'

'Then you did see me!' I broke in.

'Oh, yes, I saw you. I don't miss much.' He grinned at me sardonically, showing broken discoloured teeth. 'An' as I said, I saw little ol' Duncan too. He was down by the bridge, plodgin' in the water. I'll tell you suthin' else. It weren't your horse what knocked him down. Is that enough truth for you?'

'Oh, Mr. Pegg! Are you . . . are you

sure about this?' All I could think of just at that moment was that I was freed from guilt. The fuller implications of his words didn't hit me until later. I could have hugged him . . . greasy jacket and all!

Maybe he read my face for he stepped back and glowered at me.

'I know what I saw. I tell you, it were just an accident, thass all. Don't you go reading anythin' else into it. Mind now, this is jest between me and you an' the gatepost. If you tell anyone . . . especially the cops . . . I'll deny every word. I've mates that'll swear I wus with them all that afternoon.'

I reached out my hand to him again.

'But . . . but . . . if it wasn't my horse . . . then what . . . who . . . ?'

He interrupted me roughly.

'You don't want ter know. It's all over and done with as I said afore. Don't you go dragging it up. It won't do no good and no-one'll believe you,' and he turned and, pushing his way into the house, slammed the door in my face.

I walked back up the path in a daze. Peggy took one look at my face and got into the car while Mrs. Pegg stepped forward, twisting her hands together. I could see the worry in her pinched face.

'Mrs. Dane,' she said uncertainly, 'I'll have a word with 'im but . . . but he can be that obstinate. If it comes out that the silly ol' fule were poachin' in Thompson's wood again we'll be in real bother.'

'Don't worry. I won't get him into trouble, Mrs. Pegg. He's just taken such a load off my shoulders,' and I smiled at her joyously as I climbed into the car beside my friend.

'Well!' said Peggy, explosively, as she settled behind the wheel. 'What a wretch. Did you manage to get anything out of him? By the look on your face he must have said something.'

Mindful of Jenny on the back seat, I just nodded and said, lightly, 'Yes, yes he did. Tell you later.'

Giving me a quick glance she started

up the engine and we drove off.

'Can we just have a quick run into Fairsham, please, Pegs? We're on the way and I need to do a bit of shopping.'

'Sure. Anything you like. Do you want to go anywhere else?'

'No thanks. I badly want to talk to you . . . but, you know . . . little pigs and all that.'

'Where, Mummy?' Jenny twisted round and looked eagerly out of the window. 'Where are they?'

'Where are what, love?'

'The little pigs.'

'Now get out of that one,' chuckled Peggy and I answered her with the first lighthearted laugh that I had enjoyed for a long time, telling Jenny that she must have just missed them.

Peggy glanced at me. 'My word, Em, something's cheered you up.'

I nodded happily. 'You could say that . . .' And still the full import of his words hadn't registered. All that my mind was revelling in was that I hadn't been the one responsible for poor little

Duncan's death. For I was quite positive that Albert Pegg had told me the truth.

We did our bit of shopping and returned home and, once Peggy and I were on our own, I could contain myself no longer.

'Pegs, Albert Pegg owned up to being in the woods that afternoon and, what's more, he did see me . . . and he saw Duncan.'

'There! Shifty wretch. He wasn't going to let on, was he. It's a good job you ran after him. What made him change his mind?'

'Oh, that doesn't matter . . . but, listen, Pegs, he said it wasn't Dolly who knocked him down and somehow I'm sure he was telling the truth.'

'Did he now? Then we were right. There was someone else involved. It must have happened as we thought. Did he say who it was?'

'No, he slammed into the house then. But, Pegs, it doesn't matter. He was right about one thing. Nothing will bring little Duncan back to us but at least I know I wasn't to blame. That makes me feel so much better.'

I shook my head at her ruefully. 'The trouble is that I shan't be able to prove it to anyone else. If I tell anyone of what he has just told me he swears he will deny every word and . . . and . . .'

As I spoke, my voice faltered and I stared at Peggy, feeling a cold shiver trickling down my back.

'Emma, what's the matter? Emma?'

I must have looked as stricken as I felt for she came round to me and gave me a little shake but I couldn't speak for a moment. In my head I was back in the woods and looking up the bridle path to where the butterflies had so attracted me.

Even to me, my voice sounded far-away and strange as I answered her insistent 'Em, tell me'.

'I've just really thought about what he . . . about what Albert said. He said he'd seen Duncan playing in the shallow water by the bridge and . . . and

. . . that was just before he saw me.'

'Well?'

'Pegs, that bridge is on the other side of the wood.' I shook my head dazedly. Something was very wrong here. 'If Albert is to be believed, Duncan was much too far away to have been involved in . . . in my accident. He could never have come all that way from the bridge to where I was, in time.'

Peggy looked puzzled. 'But, Em, if Albert had time to get there then surely . . . '

I shook my head vehemently.

'No, Pegs. You see, the bridle path twists and turns and Albert was coming straight through the trees when I saw him and he was quite a long way away.' I put my hands to my face and tried to concentrate. I spoke slowly, my mind in a whirl.

'There's a lot of undergrowth. A grown man could plough his way through it but not a small boy. Albert must have seen me at about the same time that I saw him. Then he seemed to disappear into the trees like a shadow and, as far as I can remember, that was only just before my accident.'

Peggy sat very still, her eyes never leaving my face as I collected my thoughts.

'Even if Duncan had run all the way he couldn't have reached the place where it . . . it . . . happened . . . in the time.'

We stared at each other and I could see my own bewilderment mirrored in her face. At last she stirred and said slowly, 'If Albert is so sure that it wasn't your horse that knocked the child down then I think he must know a lot more than he is telling. How did poor little Duncan meet his death and also, . . . where? I was sure we'd got it right when we thought someone else was involved in your accident and I still think we are right about that. But as for Duncan . . . '

She shook her head and looked at me with alarm.

'Em, I don't like this at all.'

'Neither do I.' I felt cold and shivery and my imagination was running riot.

'Do you really think Ruth might be involved, Pegs?'

'Well, it's a possibility. But there's another thing. Supposing Albert . . . I mean, did he seem to be . . . well . . . warning you off? Do you suppose he told you that you weren't responsible for Duncan's death just to satisfy you and keep you quiet? I don't know. If there was something . . . ' She looked at me a bit desperately and I could see her hands were clenched tightly, the knuckles showing white as she burst out, 'Could he be . . . could he be . . . a danger?'

'Oh, come on, Pegs. You're being a bit dramatic here.' I didn't want to think along those lines at all.

'Well, it's that kind of situation.'

'I suppose so, but honestly, Albert didn't seem to be warning me off, as you put it. At least, I didn't get that impression.'

324

Peggy relaxed a bit but said darkly, 'Alright, Em but I still think we should be on our guard.'

'Whatever are we going to do?'

'We could go and tell the police what we know and let them sort it out.'

'But we don't *know* anything. All of it is guesswork. What could I tell them? That I have a very vague, mixed-up memory of something terrible looming up over me at the time of my accident? That a shiftless, unreliable poacher with a prison record saw me and saw the child but says I wasn't to blame? That Ruth is badly upset about something? It will just look as if I am trying to shift the blame on to someone else. Albert won't admit anything to the police. Ruth's troubles quite likely have nothing at all to do with anything and we have no proof at all.'

I looked at her worriedly.

'Maybe I'll tell Arthur about all this, tomorrow . . . or maybe I won't. I shouldn't be piling all my worries on to his shoulders. Besides, who knows what trouble we'll be stirring up . . . and perhaps for innocent people . . . if we speak to the police. Always supposing that they'll take any notice of us.'

And there we left it.

The police called at the house the next afternoon but it was just to tell me that an enquiry would be held soon and I must hold myself in readiness for it. As I opened the door to them, I was very conscious of several pairs of eyes surveying us from the village post office across the street and, rightly or wrongly, felt them to be hostile. I well knew the hierarchy. The villagers had lost one of their own. I was still a comparative newcomer and they would have closed ranks against me.

Peggy nudged me and I guessed she wanted me to tell the burly sergeant about Albert and our suspicions but I ignored her and closed the door on him as quickly as I could. After he had gone she tackled me about my 'silly scruples' as she called them.

'It's no good, Pegs,' I defended myself, 'I just don't feel justified in saying anything about Albert until I can find out more. I promise you, I will find out more, if only for Duncan's sake . . . and for Mary. But if I do give away the fact that Albert was in those woods and got him into trouble and all for nothing, I would feel terrible. Not for his sake, the wretched man,' I hurried to add, 'but for the sake of poor Mrs. Pegg and for George.'

I wrapped my one good arm around myself, feeling chilled through and through. My initial elation over the belief that perhaps, after all, I was not to blame for a little boy's death, had all but evaporated.

'Another thing, if I try to . . . to put the blame somehow on Ruth and with no proof, what is that going to achieve? Only grief for . . . for a lot of other people. No, it's best to leave things as they are for now.'

'A child has died, Emma,' said Peggy gravely, 'and it seems to me that the circumstances are suspicious.'

'Only if we believe implicitly what Albert says. He's not a reliable man, Pegs. It was an accident anyway. It couldn't have been anything else.'

I walked across to the window and stood looking out, unseeing. If Ruth had been in the woods that day . . . if she had caused the accident . . . if her stallion had been the one to kill Duncan . . . and if she was going to marry Andrew, what would the knowledge of all that do to Andrew? Far too many 'ifs'. I decided, wearily, that it would indeed be better to leave things as they were and resisted all Peggy's arguments.

But I felt torn and confused and when Jenny came running into the house, sobbing bitterly, it was the last straw. I scooped her up with my one good arm and hugged her tightly as she told me, somewhat incoherently, that two of 'the big girls' had shouted after her that her mummy was a 'bad lady'.

'You're not. You're not,' she wailed.

'Why did they say that, Mummy?'

I tried to comfort her but Peggy must have seen my bleak expression as I held her close.

'Emma, why don't I take you both back up to Manchester for a few days? Get you right away from all this for a bit. We'll have some fun and some days off all over the place. You'd love a boat ride up the canal, wouldn't you, Jenny? And I know just the place where we could do that. How about it, Em?'

Jenny gave a last hiccup and sat up, her face brightening as she nodded eagerly.

'The enquiry . . . ' I said doubtfully.

'Oh, that won't be for ages yet. We'll leave my address with the police. Dora will look after your animals for you, won't she?'

'I suppose so. But . . . but doesn't it seem a bit like running away?'

'Nonsense. It will only be for a short while anyway. Tell you what, after tea, you get your things packed and I'll pop down to see Gwen and tell them and then I'll go and see Dora for you as well. I'm sure they'll agree that a few days away would be good for you. We'll set off first thing in the morning. Just leave it all to your Auntie Pegs.'

Jenny slid off my knee, giggling.

'Ooh, Auntie Pegs, you are fun. Can I go and pack my things, Mummy. Can I take some of my toys? Can I take Heffalump?'

I looked ruefully across at my friend and spread my hands in acceptance.

'Fait accompli, Pegs. I know when to give in.'

So it was that the next morning saw the three of us set off northwards. Peggy had ridden over every obstacle, letting Gwen and Arthur and the Rawdons know of our plans and arranging for Dora to keep an eye on the house and take in Tabitha and Jess.

'Why, of course,' she had said, when asked 'They know me. Tabitha was born here after all and they'll be company for me.'

'I'm being so useless,' I complained

but Peggy just laughed.

'You're not up to scratch yet, my girl. Don't worry, you'll be your own bossy self again before long.'

'How you, of all people, can say that!' and I found myself laughing.

I gave my little home a last look before we turned the corner out of the village and unwelcome questions slipped across my mind. Would I come back? Would I be able to go on living and working here under the circumstances. Just a few weeks ago I had been so happy and now ... I shivered and resolutely turned to face forward, fighting back incipient tears. Whatever lay ahead of me I knew I was blessed in having my darling Jenny and some good and loving friends. I eased my sling into a more comfortable position and lifted my chin a fraction higher.

11

I expected to feel a kind of home-coming, walking into Peggy's house, but although it was still exactly as I remembered it, it felt strange and, unreasonably, all I wanted to do was to turn round and go straight back to Norfolk. Sighing, I pulled myself together, aware that Peggy was doing her level best to help me. We unpacked and settled ourselves in and, while sitting around the electric fire that evening . . . oh, how I missed the leaping flames of my log fire . . . I spoke of the possibility of giving up my job at Little Croxfield.

'I've given it a great deal of thought, Pegs and I can't see any other option. I just cannot see how I can possibly be freed from blame. Whatever we may have thought about . . . about someone else being involved it is still only pure conjecture and we . . . I . . . can't really do anything about it. I shall still feel responsible and how can I live there with that hanging over my head always? And what about Jenny? That nasty little experience she had might very well be the first of many. I daren't risk that. There are . . . are other reasons too.'

I stared into the glowing bars in the hearth trying to banish Andrew's face from my mind. With remarkably little success.

If Peggy guessed what those other reasons were she made no comment but just shook her head sympathetically.

'It's such a shame. You were really happy there, weren't you, Em? Jenny too. Would you come back to Manchester?'

'Oh, no. I'll look round for somewhere else in Norfolk. It's a big county and there will probably be other posts far enough away.' My voice faltered. 'You probably think I'm running away and I suppose I am. But I just can't live there any longer as . . . as . . . as things are and . . . and, thinking of little Duncan and always wondering if I had killed him.'

Peggy looked horrified and started to speak but I held up my hand to her.

'I know what you're going to say. That it was an accident. But what if it was? It was still an accident that I must have caused. I must have been careless not to have avoided him. I've thought and thought about what Albert Pegg said and I really don't know if I can trust him. Perhaps he did only say what he did to . . . oh, I don't know . . . make me feel better for some reason . . . or . . . or get me off his back. I feel so terribly mixed up.'

I folded my arms awkwardly and hugged them to me, trying to control an insistent, shivery feeling.

'I still can't remember exactly what happened that afternoon and perhaps I never will. If I am responsible for Duncan's death then I will have to live with that for the rest of my life. Everyone in Croxfield will be bound to blame me and . . . and I suppose I am a coward but honestly, Pegs, I just don't think I can take that. And what about Jenny? It will affect her too and that is more important than anything. No, while I'm up here, I shall have to write to Douglas and give in my notice.'

'Well, I can understand how you feel but don't do anything about it yet, Em,' was Peggy's advice. 'Give yourself a breathing space.'

She got out of her chair to turn up the fire and attempted to change the subject.

'That Mrs. Bruce. Isn't she a nice woman? She's given you a lot of support hasn't she?'

'Yes, she's been marvellous,' I agreed but I felt my face stiffen as she continued.

'What about Andrew? I gather he's been away but surely he's heard all about it by now? I thought he and you were . . . well . . . such good friends?'

'He's still away,' I said shortly. 'He knows nothing.'

'But surely his mother will be telling him all about it as soon as she can?' Peggy persisted.

'Believe me, Pegs, he won't want to know.' I turned away from her questioning look and added, 'Please, Pegs, I . . . I don't want to talk about it,' and although I had tried to keep my voice matter-of-fact, I felt that I must have sounded a shade desperate for she said no more.

But I was wrong. So very wrong.

We watched a film on television for the rest of the evening but I don't think either of us could have said what it was about when we finally switched off and went to bed.

The next day dawned bright and sunny but I couldn't help comparing the quality of Manchester's blue skies with those I had left behind. Even the air felt different. Peggy laughed at me when I exaggerated and said I couldn't breathe but it wasn't really so far from the truth.

We took Jenny for her canal ride,

pottered around the shops for a bit and treated ourselves to a meal out. My arm was still giving me a certain amount of pain and discomfort and I confess I used this as an excuse for my lack of enthusiasm. Once back at Peggy's house, I sank into an armchair with some relief. Jenny was in the kitchen with Peggy, chattering away happily and I put my head back and shut my eyes. I really must pull myself together, I told myself firmly. I must be strong, for Jenny's sake. But I wish . . . my thoughts tailed off for I didn't want to think too closely of what I was wishing for.

Peggy came in then and I opened my eyes and looked at the clock.

'Jenny, love, it's past your bedtime,' I called and began to struggle out of the chair.

'Stay where you are. I'll give her a hand.' Peggy's voice was firm and equally as firm was Jenny's 'I can wash myself, Mummy.' So I laughed and gave up with very little resistance.

There seemed to be a great deal of splashing and giggling coming from the bathroom and I found myself grinning and losing some of the tension that had held me in its grip.

'Have you both enjoyed yourselves?' I asked lazily as they came downstairs, Jenny rosy and scrubbed in her teddy-bear pyjamas and Peggy, liberally splashed and decidedly rumpled.

Neither had the chance to answer for at that moment the doorbell rang and Peggy went to answer it, muttering crossly and running a hand through her dishevelled hair.

I heard voices coming from the hall and shook my head in disbelief. It couldn't be . . . could it? Pushing myself up out of my chair, I turned towards the doorway. I could feel my heart pounding and I could hardly breathe. I certainly couldn't have moved a step.

Peggy came back into the room followed by a familiar, tall, broad-shouldered figure and I could only stand like a fool and stare.

Jenny had no such inhibitions.

'Uncle Andrew!' she shrieked and flung herself at him. 'Oh, I wanted you!' . . . Which were exactly my sentiments too.

He bent down to pick her up and hug her as if it were the most natural thing in the world for him to do and his eyes met mine across the top of her curly head. He looked anxious and unsure of himself.

Keeping Jenny in his arms, almost as if she was a lifeline, he looked down at Peggy.

'I hope it's alright to barge in here like this?' he asked.

She gave me a quizzical look and answered dryly, 'Judging by the welcome you've just had and the one you're about to get, I would think it's quite alright.'

'Peggy!' I felt my face grow warm. 'We're pleased to see you, of course, Andrew.' I know my voice must have sounded stilted. 'But what . . . I mean, why . . . we weren't expecting . . . ' I floundered to a halt.

Quickly, Peggy came to my rescue.

'Of course you're welcome. Now Jenny, let Mr. Bruce put you down and then he can sit down and have a cup of coffee?'

Jenny reluctantly let go her stranglehold and was put down and my knees suddenly gave way and I sank back into my chair.

'Coffee would be very welcome Miss . . . er . . . Mitchell. Is that right?'

She shook her head at him, smiling. 'Peggy would be better and you're Andrew, aren't you? Jenny, love, will you come and help me make your Uncle Andrew and the rest of us some coffee?'

She whisked Jenny away and I heard them discussing the merits of chocolate biscuits before she finally shut the kitchen door.

For what seemed to be a long, long moment we looked at each other. Maybe we were both remembering the last time we had spoken. But there was no angry, bitter look on his face this time. In fact, he still appeared to be decidedly uncertain. He spread his hands on his knees and, looking down at them, began to speak.

'I've been away, walking. Did Ma tell you?'

'Yes,' I whispered.

'I did a lot of thinking and . . . and . . . ' he hesitated and I realised incredulously that he was actually nervous.

'Emma, I've been such a stupid, jealous fool.' He looked up then, 'Forgive me, . . . please. When Ma told me of all you had been through, I . . . well, all I wanted to do was come and . . . and see if you were alright. Are you alright, Emma?'

'Oh, yes,' I answered, my heart singing. He had come to find me. Never mind that there had been misunderstandings . . . never mind that bitter words had been spoken. I had needed him so much . . . and here he was.

My face must have given me away for he gave a kind of groan and was out of his chair and kneeling on the floor in front of me and I was enfolded in a strong and loving hug. Hampered as I was by my sling, I still managed to wrap my arms around him and turn my face for his kiss.

One reads about bells ringing and music playing and even the earth moving at such times. Believe me, they are only poor descriptions.

'Then you are glad to see me?' he asked at last. 'I wasn't sure what my reception would be after the way I have behaved but I had to come. Oh, my poor darling, I am so sorry, so very sorry.'

'Hush,' I said and had to kiss my forgiveness as he rocked me in his arms . . . which of course led to more words of endearment and further kisses.

I heard Peggy call from the kitchen, 'Jenny, will you come back and carry this plate for me?' and hurriedly we disentangled ourselves and Andrew just had time to step in front of the fireplace as Jenny came in, importantly carrying a plate of biscuits with Peggy close behind her with the coffee.

'Can I get you something to eat?' asked Peggy. 'You've had a long journey.'

'Thank you, but I stopped for a meal on the way here,' he replied. 'I'm fine.'

'When did you get back from Yorkshire?' I asked.

'Early this afternoon.' He grinned wryly as I exclaimed in horror.

'You mean to say that you turned round and came all the way back up north again. Oh, Andrew!'

'And I'm afraid I mustn't stay too long either. I've got to get back to Norfolk tonight.'

Peggy and I both joined in protesting about this but he was adamant.

'I know we've got a lot to talk about, Emma but most of it can wait. You'll be coming home soon, won't you?'

I looked at him then, in despair, my euphoria slipping away and slowly shook my head.

'Look,' said Peggy quickly. 'Let me take Jenny up to bed and then you can have some time to talk before Andrew has to go back. Emma?'

'Thank you, Pegs,' I said gratefully and turned to Jenny who was beginning to look downcast. 'Go along, sweetheart, there's a good girl. Say goodnight to Uncle Andrew and I'll be up shortly.'

She heaved a big sigh and trailed across to him and he bent down for her goodnight kiss.

'I'll read you a story,' said Peggy, diplomatically. 'Which one shall it be?'

Jenny's face lit up. 'Oh, goody. Paddington Bear please, Auntie Pegs,' and the two of them disappeared upstairs.

Andrew leaned forward and looked at me intently.

'Are you really sure you're alright, Emma? How is your head now? When I heard you had been unconscious for three days, I was so worried. Your poor arm, too.' He shook his head at me.

'Oh, I'm fine and getting better every day,' I answered airily.

'Why did you shake your head when I asked about you coming home? That doesn't sound fine to me,' and those keen, dark blue eyes fixed me with a look that seemed to see right through into my troubled mind.

'Oh, Andrew, it is all such a mess,' I began. 'I just don't know what to do.'

'Try telling me all about it,' he said quietly. 'That's why I'm here ... to help, if I can.'

I glanced at him gratefully and endeavoured to get my chaotic thoughts into some sort of order. But how could I tell him everything without telling him of our suspicions concerning Ruth? And how would he handle that? ... Ruth! ... I thought. If he is really involved with her, what on earth made him come flying up here to find me and ... and what about those kisses? They had certainly been more ... much more ... than just friendly ones. I looked across at him, even more

345

troubled and he must have seen my uncertainty for he moved his chair closer and took my hand.

'Start at the beginning,' he said and smiled down at me. 'It's always the best place. Ma only gave me the bare bones of everything, as you might say.'

So I did just that and I had just got to the part where Gwen and Peggy had come to fetch me out of hospital, when Peggy came downstairs.

'Jenny wants you to go and say goodnight to her,' she said, after listening for a minute or two. So I went upstairs and, although I was as quick as possible, by the time I got down again it was obvious that Peggy had been filling in a few details that I would have preferred to have left out.

'Pegs!' I said quickly. 'Don't bother Andrew with all those conjectures of ours. They might not mean a thing.'

She ignored me and turned to Andrew, looking at him keenly.

'Do you really want to help Emma?' she asked abruptly.

'More than anything,' he answered straightly and she gave a satisfied nod.

'Then we must tell you every little detail and you can judge for yourself.'

I put out my hand to restrain her. 'Peggy, please.'

But my friend was always the blunt one. Straight to the point and no messing.

'I know what's bothering Emma,' she said. 'She's afraid of involving your . . . your fiancée,' and her voice had an unspoken question in it.

Andrew looked utterly astounded.

'My fiancée? what on earth are you talking about? I haven't got a fiancée.'

I broke in, feeling a great deal of embarrassment. I could cheerfully have strangled my best and dearest friend.

'I thought . . . well . . . that you and Ruth . . . were going to . . . to get engaged.'

He threw his head back and gave a shout of laughter.

'Good grief! Absolutely no way. Besides, I've always thought of her as a kind of kid sister.'

When I thought of all my misery . . . and he sat there, laughing . . . I could cheerfully have strangled him too.

My brief fit of pique soon disappeared and, between us, Peggy and I told him every detail we could think of about my disastrous accident and all that had happened since. As the story unfolded his face grew sad and stern and I faltered in the telling more than once, remembering that after all, Bill and Ruth Thompson had been his friends for years.

We came to the end of our story and my restless fingers fiddled with my empty coffee cup. I couldn't bear the look of strain on his face.

'Andrew, we're probably snatching at straws here,' I said, desperately but he shook his head slowly and his forehead creased in thought.

'No, Emma, I'm very much afraid that Peggy is right. There is certainly a great deal more to this affair than we know of.'

'I didn't want you to know,' I muttered miserably and he turned and looked at me keenly.

'Emma, if someone else is involved in all this then we must find out who. I won't have you blamed.'

My sore heart lifted a little and I made an effort and smiled at him waveringly.

He nodded encouragingly and then, apropos of nothing we had just been talking of, added, 'Whatever made you suppose that Ruth and I were engaged?'

'She told me,' I said simply, 'At the Norfolk Show Day. She even showed me the ring you had bought her.'

He looked stunned. 'What ring?'

'It was a gorgeous great emerald.' I said shortly . . . for the memory of that day still rankled.

He shook his head in disbelief.

'Nothing to do with me.'

He still looked astounded and then I could see comprehension dawning in his eyes.

'A fairly large emerald, with diamonds at each side?'

I nodded coolly.

'The little minx! Her father gave her that for her eighteenth birthday. She was flashing it all over the place to all and sundry.'

I heard an indrawn breath behind me from Peggy and then she broke in, swiftly.

'Tell Andrew about that note, Em.'

I looked at her doubtfully. 'Peggy, I don't . . . '

'Oh, Em! Then I will. Andrew, Emma found a piece of screwed up paper in her garden when she came back from the Show. It puzzled us because it looked as if it was part of a note that . . . that could have been pinned to her gate. I suppose you can't throw any light on it? You see it rather looked as if the note had been addressed to you.'

She studied him with her head on one side and fairly quivering with expectancy. She reminded me irresistibly of Jess when she is on a hunt and I felt a grin bubbling up. Stealing a glance at Andrew, that grin died a very quick death for his face had darkened.

'Yes,' he said curtly. 'I could throw some light on that note . . . if I chose to.'

'Right then,' said Peggy cheerfully, 'You jolly well choose to, my lad. This is a time for telling all.'

I could see that, in spite of himself, Andrew was amused at her breeziness and he pushed his hair back off his forehead and a betraying twinkle took the darkness from his eyes. He told his side of the misunderstanding which had so marred that day and we began to realise the extent of Ruth's scheming. When we pieced everything together we realised that she must have been responsible for the bogus emergency call in which a dog had been supposedly injured and, knowing that he would never ignore such a thing, rung him immediately afterwards to offer him a lift to the show.

'I told her I had to go on this call and

asked her to stop by your house and explain and ask you to wait.' Andrew ran his hands through his hair again. He seemed to do this in times of stress, I had noticed and my hand almost reached out of its own accord to smooth it . . . and his confusion . . . away.

'When I finally reached your house,' he continued, ' . . . and I must confess I was more than a bit annoyed to have been sent on a wild-goose chase . . . it was to find your note pinned to the gate, telling me that you had no intention of waiting for me and that you had gone off with Bill Thompson instead,' and he scowled.

'Not my note, Andrew,' I said cheerfully, for now I was seeing clearly through Ruth's deceit. 'I'm afraid that was another red herring.'

Eventually we sorted it all out between us . . . and another small load dropped off my shoulders.

'Look,' he said at last, 'I really will have to make tracks. When I get home I shall certainly take that young lady to task for her actions on the Show Day.' He hesitated for a moment and then sighed and shrugged his shoulders. 'And if she has somehow been involved with . . . well, with your accident, I promise you, Emma that I will do what I can to find out the truth of it all. Try not to worry. If heaven and earth have to be moved . . . then I'll do it. But you must come back. Please don't take any drastic steps yet.'

'That's what I told her,' agreed Peggy.

'Well, I shall have to come back for the hearing, anyway,' I said, unhappily.

Peggy spoke comfortingly.

'Perhaps it will all have been cleared up by then.'

Andrew nodded agreement and then jumped to his feet.

'I'll ring you tomorrow. Emma . . . and promise that you'll come back soon?'

Wordlessly, I nodded and Peggy tactfully bustled off to the front door, leaving us alone. He reached out and took both my hands in his, gazing down at me.

'Emma, I really am so sorry that you are in this trouble. I promise you I will do all I can to help and . . . and I'm sorry that I've been so . . . '

'Hush' I said and put my fingers on his lips. 'Let's forget all that.'

'Friends, then?'

'Of course,' and I smiled up at him happily.

'Remember, don't think any more about handing your notice in. I know it may not be easy for you at first but you'll be surprised at how soon this part of your life will recede to the background. You will feel the same about poor little Duncan wherever you go, but it wasn't your fault love. I'd stake my life on that. You are so well thought of in the village already, Emma. The people there won't want to lose you.'

My face must have been still troubled for he reached out and gently stroked my hair away from the livid bruises that were still showing on my forehead.

'My poor darling. Believe me. The gossip will soon be forgotten. You know what village life is like. This will all be a nine day's wonder and then they'll find something else to talk about. All your friends will rally round you.'

He wrapped his arms around me and held me close. Then bent his head . . . and his kiss was sweetness and glory . . . and far too short.

After Peggy and I had waved him off and closed the door, she turned to me and said, with a perfectly straight face,

'Do you know, I could have sworn I heard the jingle of harness and the galloping of hooves just then!'

I stared at her, uncomprehendingly, for a moment and then she dissolved in laughter.

'Oh, Em! Your face! It was just your knight in shining armour riding off to do battle, that's all.'

'You fool, Pegs.'

I gave her a hug and we linked arms

affectionately, as we went back, light-heartedly, into the sitting room.

I was on tenterhooks the next day, waiting for Andrew's call, wondering if I could possibly have misconstrued any of his words or actions. My self-confidence was at a very low ebb in those days. When at last the phone rang, I backed away and called for Peggy to come and answer it. She lifted the receiver and then rolled her eyes, expressively.

'She's just here, Andrew,' she said and held it out to me.

'Mummy, Mummy, can I talk to Uncle Andrew?'

An eager little hand tugged at my arm.

'Well, just for a minute. He's phoning from a long way away and won't have a lot of time.'

But I was glad of the moment to collect myself while she asked after Old Moke. She would have gone through the entire list of pets and patients if I hadn't retrieved the phone with a certain degree of firmness.

He didn't have much to tell me, of course, but it was just so good to hear his voice.

'Ma and Dad send their love,' he concluded. 'And we want to know when you are coming back. You might not have heard this yet but I believe the enquiry is scheduled for next week.'

'I'd better come home at the weekend then. Jenny and I will catch the train on Saturday.'

'If you can wait until Sunday, I'll come up and fetch you. You don't want to be struggling with luggage and a small girl, on and off trains, with your arm in a sling.'

I started to protest but he was adamant.

'Emma, love, I'm not listening. Ma would never forgive me and Dad would disown me. I'll give you another ring some time on Saturday, if that's O.K.?'

I agreed, glowing at the 'love', owning to myself, ruefully, that all my resolutions about not ever getting involved with another man were fast flying out of the window. It also occurred to me that I had used the words 'come home' without a second thought.

Peggy had offered to drive me back to Norfolk when the time came but her holiday in Italy was getting ever closer and I knew she would have lots to do so I had assured her that we would be fine on the train. I must admit that Andrew's suggestion was very welcome and I hugged myself at the thought of seeing him again soon . . . although I was certainly not looking forward to the enquiry.

I woke early on Sunday morning and lay for a while, reluctant to get up and start the day for I had been anticipating it with mixed feelings. I longed to see Andrew again and Gwen and Arthur who had become like family to me. I yearned for my own little home . . . and yet . . . and yet . . . I was afraid of returning to what the next few days might throw at me. I thought this through, burrowing down under the comforting warmth of the duvet. It was when I owned up to myself that I was afraid that I found the nerve to throw back the covers and swing my feet to the floor. 'Wimp!' I censured myself, 'Face up to things.' I thought of what poor Mary had to face and felt ashamed.

I knew I had to go back and deal with everything as best I could. I'll follow Peggy's good advice, I thought and leave all major decisions for the time being. I hurriedly showered and dressed, feeling much better and by then the others were up and it was time to get breakfast on the way. Gwen had phoned the night before to explain that Andrew had been called out so she was ringing for him to say that he would arrive to pick us up at mid-day.

He arrived earlier but we hadn't much to pack so we were ready and waiting. Peggy gave me a hug and made me promise to phone her as soon as she had returned from her holiday.

'I might phone you myself,' she said, 'Before then.'

'What, all the way from Italy?' I cried. 'Don't you dare. Now, I shall be O.K. Pegs. Don't worry.'

'We shall look after the both of them.' Andrew assured her and bent down to strap Jenny into the back seat.

I gave Peggy one last hug. 'Thanks for everything, pal. I don't know what I'd have done without you. Have a lovely time in Italy.'

Once in the car, I leaned out of the window to look up at her and made myself chuckle.

'I bet you'll be really glad to get away from all the drama!'

She flapped a dismissive hand at me and grinned.

'It will be a rest cure!'

'Ready?' Andrew turned and looked down at me and I nodded and smiled as widely as I could and if he noticed that it was a little forced, he made no comment but just reached out and gripped my hand and gave it a little shake.

'Right. Off we go then. 'Bye Peggy.'

With a chorus of 'goodbyes' we all waved until we had turned the corner.

12

I sat quietly as Andrew negotiated us out of Manchester's busy streets but I did notice that he seemed to be a little on edge. Well, not exactly on edge, I suppose, more excited. Several times he seemed to be on the verge of speaking and then gave a quick glance into the mirror in front of him and I realised that he was looking to where Jenny was busy undressing her doll and changing her clothes. Then he either closed his mouth again or made some commonplace remark. Not until we had left the city far behind did he lean towards me and say quietly,

'I've got some great news for you, Emma. There's such a lot to tell you.'

'I thought there was something. You've been like a cat on hot bricks ever since we got in the car.'

He laughed. 'Was it that obvious?

Well, I can't wait to tell you any longer and I think our Jenny has dropped off. I was hoping she would.'

With some difficulty I twisted round to see that my small daughter was indeed fast asleep.

'I can't say I'm surprised. She was so excited at the thought of going back to Croxfield that she didn't get to sleep until very late last night. Well, what is it then?'

'You're off the hook, Emma. You didn't have anything to do with Duncan's death. Albert Pegg is going to give evidence at the enquiry to prove this.'

His voice was exultant.

I couldn't believe my ears. 'Oh, Andrew! What happened to make him change his mind? Did you speak to him? Oh, tell me . . . I can't believe it.'

My voice rose and I abruptly hushed it, for now was not the time to wake Jenny.

'You just sit back and listen and I'll tell you it all from the beginning.'

And so he told me of how he had gone round to speak to Albert, determined to get the truth out of him and succeeded beyond his most eager hopes.

'When I got to the Pegg's house,' he began, 'Albert was out but Mrs. Pegg was there and she was a bit wary at first. When I said I had to see him and it was very important, she grabbed hold of my sleeve and asked if it was about you. So, of course, I said yes and she almost dragged me down the garden path and round to the back of the house, talking away about how she knew what he'd been up to and how he was going to get himself into trouble again and cause them all such hardship . . . and on and on. The poor woman seemed almost beside herself. We ended up outside their garden shed and there she stopped and seemed to gather herself together.'

'I want to help Mrs. Dane,' she said, 'and I know that Albert was in the woods the day of her accident and saw a lot more than he will let on.'

'Too true!' I broke in. 'I know he saw me because he owned up to that but he wouldn't tell me any more . . . except that he did say that I wasn't to blame. Oh, Andrew, was he really telling the truth after all?' and I twisted round and looked up at him eagerly.

He nodded and smiled. 'Patience . . . hang on . . . all will be revealed. Just listen.'

So I gave an impatient sigh and listened intently.

'Mrs. Pegg then said that she knew of a way to make him talk and I wondered just what I was getting into! 'If I tell you,' she said, 'and what he says puts Mrs. Dane in the clear, will you promise to keep quiet about what he's done?'

"Of course, I had to say that depended on just what the blighter had been up to but she assured me that it wasn't anything very dreadful. Just something that would get him into trouble with old Thompson, so I guessed it was probably poaching or something like that, so in the end, I promised. I know that he and Bill's father have been enemies for years and Mr. Thompson has sworn to get him sent to prison if he can.

"She flung open the shed door and at the far end was what looked like a pile of sacks. 'Go and have a look,' she said, so I pulled off the top sack and there was the biggest pile of pheasants and rabbits that you ever did see. All neatly trussed together and obviously waiting for delivery. 'He's gone to get his pal's van,' she said, 'to take this lot to . . . well . . . to where it's going. If you tell him you know about this I reckon you can make him say what you want. Especially if you say you'll tell old Thompson. He would be in trouble then.'

'Apparently she had thought of holding this knowledge over his head herself but then had second thoughts and that was why she had been so pleased to see me.'

'She's scared of him, poor little

woman,' I told him. 'Albert Pegg can be quite a bully.'

'Mmm. I gathered that. Anyway, I had a good idea then. I always carry a camera in the car. With my job, it can be quite useful for reference. So I nipped back and got it and took a couple of shots of his pile of booty. You know, Emma, when I examined those birds, none of them had been shot. I had wondered about that.'

'How on earth did he get them then?'

'Crafty old blighter! Thompson's gamekeeper had bred quite a flock of them for the shoot and they were reasonably tame.'

'Oh, I do think that's awful,' I broke in, hotly. 'Rearing those beautiful birds just to shoot at them.'

He reached across and patted my hand. 'Yes, love, I agree with you but it's what happens, I'm afraid and Albert took advantage of it.'

He returned his hand to the steering wheel and I possessed my soul in patience.

'What Albert had done, I suspect, is an old trick. He'd soaked corn in whisky and scattered it about near the pheasant pens. The birds had gone there to be fed and eaten Albert's corn and got roaring drunk! It's easy enough then to pick them up and wring their necks.'

I looked at him, unbelievingly, but he just nodded.

'Oh, yes, I'm pretty sure that's what he did. The rabbits, of course, were snared and that's illegal too. Anyway, as I was saying, I took these photographs as proof and then Mrs. Pegg turned up trumps. She pointed out that a photograph of a pile of pheasants really proved nothing unless you knew where they were. 'If I stand by the shed door and point at them,' she said, 'and you take another photo, that'll prove who had them.' She can be sharp enough at times.'

'I think it was very brave of her,' I added. 'Goodness knows what Albert will do when he finds out.'

'Ah, well, I can tell you exactly what Albert did because he rolled up just as I was putting my camera back in the car. I taxed him with everything and he blustered a bit and then all his bravado collapsed like a pricked balloon when I told him of the photographs. He started to roar at the poor little woman but I told him that if I ever heard one word about him ill-treating her in any way, then those photographs would go straight to Mr. Thompson. The main thing is that he will go to the enquiry and say what he saw in the wood. But listen to this, Emma. He not only saw you ambling along, as you said, but he also saw Ruth, galloping towards you hell-for-leather and crash into you just as you turned the corner.'

'I knew it,' I said in a whisper. 'That terrible blackness . . . and those teeth! Oh, Andrew . . . Ruth's great stallion!'

'Yes.' His voice had become sombre. 'It always was a fearsome brute.'

He was quiet for a bit, negotiating a

busy roundabout and I waited, breath-lessly, for the next bit of the story and when I stole a look at him, I guessed by his face that his thoughts were not happy ones. Once we were in calm traffic again, I reached across and gave his shoulder a little encouraging pat.

'Please go on, Andrew. What hap-pened then? Did Ruth see Albert?'

'No, apparently not. Albert said he was watching from the shelter of some bushes and saw Ruth dismount and bend over you as you lay on the ground. Then she stood up and seemed to be thinking what to do . . . at least, that's the impression he got . . . before she flung herself back into the saddle and rode back the way she had come.'

With my voice a mere thread, I asked what was to me the crucial question.

'And . . . and . . . Duncan?'

I saw his knuckles whiten as he gripped the steering wheel tighter.

'That's the strangest part, Emma. Albert waited until Ruth was out of sight and then came out of his hiding place and went over to you. He said there was no sign of Duncan at all. Dolly was still standing there at the side of the path although she was obviously distressed . . . but no Duncan.'

My senses swam and I gasped, 'But, Andrew, when the police found me they . . . they . . . found Duncan lying at the side of me. Is Albert sure about this?'

'Yes, positive. He saw you were unconscious but said that as he was sure that Ruth had gone for help there wasn't anything he could do, so he made himself scarce. You should have heard Mrs. Pegg when he told us that. She called him all the names under the sun for not going for help or at least staying with you until help came.'

I remembered Albert's words about seeing the little boy playing by the bridge and thinking that it would have been well nigh impossible for the child to have reached me and reminded Andrew of this.

'I know, Emma. I've given that some thought too. In fact just before I came to fetch you home I took Major along that path and worked out distances and there is only one answer.'

He turned his head and our eyes met. His held a great sadness and mine a dawning horror.

'It can only mean that Duncan was killed somewhere else and his body was put by you as you lay unconscious.'

'So that I would be blamed,' I whispered, aghast.

'I'm afraid so, love.'

'You think it was Ruth, don't you?'

'It points that way. She was there at the crucial time and it was a horse's kick that killed the child.'

'They might be wrong about that. It could have been someone else. Anybody could have been in the woods that day.'

But he shook his head sadly.

We both sat, wordless, for a long while and then, out of my shock and dismay came a feeling of dawning relief . . . and a realisation that Peggy had been right after all.

I also realised that it was all very well but so far we only had Albert's word for this. Would it be accepted at the enquiry?

As if he had read my uneasy thoughts, Andrew shifted in his seat and flexed his shoulders as if to rid himself of tension.

'I went over to Thompson's farm yesterday,' he said quietly. 'Bill told me that Ruth had gone away to stay with an aunt. He seemed quite unlike himself and I knew something was wrong but he didn't confide in me. All he would say was that his father had gone to fetch Ruth home. So we must wait until they return and then see what Ruth knows about all this.'

'She never went to get help for me . . . or for Duncan,' I said, unhappily. 'Dolly returned alone and in a bad state and that was why the search party was sent out.'

'I know . . . and Dad told me about the weal on Dolly's hindquarters.'

'I wish Ruth didn't hate me so.'

I gulped and bent my head, searching frantically for a handkerchief.

'Oh, Emma, love. Don't be upset. Oh, Hell!' He reached out to hold my hand. 'Look, there's a service station coming up. We'll stop for a break. Come on, sweetheart. Everything's going to be alright.'

I blew my nose, scrubbed at my face and managed a watery smile. Jenny clambered sleepily out of the car and we went in search of that age-old British comforter . . . a cup of tea.

The rest of the journey home was uneventful. Jenny was wide awake so we kept from the subject that was occupying all my thoughts . . . and, I suspect . . . Andrew's as well.

As we drove into Little Croxfield, I saw a straggling group of people standing about in the street near the schoolhouse. Most of them were the parents of some of my school children but I noticed a sprinkling of the older villagers as well. They came up and crowded round as the car came to a stop and Jenny and I got out.

'Thass it, my woman . . . ' 'Glad to have you back . . . ' 'Are you alright then?'

These words and many others rang in my ears and I felt my arms and shoulders being patted hesitantly. Everyone was smiling and then a small girl was pushed forward . . . one of Jenny's classmates . . . with a large bunch of flowers.

I turned towards them and I know my voice was choked as I thanked them all.

'Oh, thank you. How very nice of you all. Yes, yes, I'm glad to be . . . to be home.'

They waved again and drifted away, chattering and I looked across at Andrew, who was leaning on the top of the car watching me, his face bright with laughter.

'You see? I told you they wouldn't want to lose you, Emma.'

'But . . . but . . . do they know, Andrew? How on earth . . . ?'

'If you mean, do they know that you

are free from blame, then, yes. Judging by your reception, I think they must.'

He turned and held open my gate and I walked through and looked up the path. There in the open doorway stood Gwen and Jenny ran ahead to be picked up and hugged.

'Well!' she said briskly. 'Wasn't that a nice welcome? Come along in my dears. Dora is here as well, making the tea and Jess and Tabitha can't wait to see you again,' and Jenny was put down to run off and be reunited with the animals, while I was greeted with a warm and loving kiss in my turn.

I was still marvelling at the attitude of the village people when Dora bustled in with the teapot.

'Humph!' she exclaimed, putting it down with a thump. 'They should've been like that afore. When you needed it most.'

'Oh, Dora, you can't blame them. What I don't understand is why they have suddenly changed their attitude.'

'Because now they know the truth.

Well, some on it anyhow. That there Aggie Pegg has been tellin' all her cronies about her Albert being in the woods that day. I reckon there's a bit more to it than that, though. He'd a'bin up to mischief, I'll be bound and she must ha' got summat on him to make her so cocky. No-one's ever seen her get the upper hand on him afore . . . not since the day he wed her,' and she sniffed scornfully and poured the tea.

Andrew and I exchanged a small secret smile.

I was informed that the public enquiry would be held on the following Friday and the days in between seemed to drag never-endingly.

It was held in a large room in the council office building in Fairsham and Gwen and Arthur and Andrew all went with me. My staunch little friend, Dora was looking after Jenny, who, fortunately, was quite oblivious of the drama unfolding. There was quite a crowd at the back of the room as it was a public enquiry and I shivered at the thought of all the interest the affair was arousing and the possible publicity.

The police gave their account first and then I was asked to give mine. Knowing now that I wasn't to blame gave me the confidence to speak calmly and tell of my experience with an easy heart. When Albert was called there was a rustle and a murmuring from the public seats and I looked across and caught Mrs. Pegg's eye. She nodded at me, encouragingly but I noticed that she kept her glances away from Albert, who was looking even more malevolent than usual. As he stood, he turned his head and gave Andrew a look, which, to me, was full of meaning but Andrew merely leaned back a little more in his chair, with his arms folded and regarded him blandly.

There was a concerted gasp from all corners of the room when Albert stated that there had been no sign of little Duncan anywhere when he, Albert, had come out of the bushes to find me lying unconscious on the ground.

'Are you sure about this?' asked the coroner. 'Are you quite sure he wasn't perhaps lying somewhere in the vicinity?'

'He weren't lyin' in anywhere,' said Albert, truculently. 'I'd a'seen him, had he a' been. I never saw 'im no more arter I saw 'im along by the river. I knows what I saw.'

There was a kind of disturbance at the back of the room and a stern voice made itself heard over the growing whispers and mutterings.

'Aye, and he attempts to put his knowledge to good use . . . or rather bad use . . . the scoundrel.'

Mr. Thompson made his way through the gathering, only coming to a halt when he reached the long table behind which the coroner sat.

'I apologise for interrupting your proceedings, sir,' he said firmly. 'But I . . . we . . . have some vital evidence which affects this enquiry.'

Only a little way behind him was Ruth and I couldn't take my eyes off her. She was, as always, dressed smartly and her tan linen suit complemented that glorious auburn hair. But her face was white and drawn and there were bruising shadows beneath her eyes. There was no other word for it . . . she looked haunted. My initial anger at the sight of her began to dissipate and as I began to imagine what an ordeal was possibly ahead of her, it dissolved into pity. Andrew stirred uneasily, next to me and I know we were both wondering what disclosures the next few moments would bring. Neither of us had an inkling of the whole of it however.

The coroner nodded towards the burly man standing before him.

'Mr. Thompson, isn't it? Well, we can certainly do with some clarification of this issue. Please sit down over there, sir,' and he gestured towards two seats on the other side of Arthur's wheel-chair, 'and we'll hear your information shortly.'

He turned back to Albert, who had been glaring at Mr. Thompson defiantly.

I thought it was to do with that pile of pheasants secreted in his shed . . . but I was wrong.

He gave the last of his evidence and then hurriedly made his way to the door. For some reason there were two strapping policemen standing there, barring his way and after a bit of a scuffle and loud complaints and a few curses from Albert, he was persuaded, none too gently, into a chair with a policeman on either side of him.

The buzz of speculating voices grew to fever pitch and I turned to Andrew in dismayed surprise.

'What was all that about? It was a shade drastic for a bit of poaching, wasn't it?'

'I've no idea. There must be something more.'

The coroner called for order and asked Mr. Thompson to stand and in the ensuing hush, you could have heard the proverbial pin drop.

'Now Mr. Thompson, what have you to tell this enquiry?'

Jack Thompson swung round and pointed a finger at Albert, who was, at last, silent and sullen.

'That blackguard still hasn't told you all he knows. But I can.'

He turned back to face the stern figure behind the desk.

'He's told you about one accident that he witnessed but he hasn't told you the whole truth about that poor little boy.'

His shoulders sagged and he paused for a moment to take a deep breath before continuing.

'Apparently, after taking a look at Mrs. Dane, he made off through the woods, back towards the bridge. He saw my daughter there . . . and he saw Duncan again but this time the poor little fellow was dead. There wasn't much doubt about it.'

I gave a gasp and clutched at Andrew's arm. We all sat as if stunned.

Jack Thompson pulled out a hankerchief and rubbed it across his face and his voice hardened.

'When he heard the circumstances of Mrs. Dane's accident he put two and two together and then, three days ago, the swine came to blackmail me. He offered to keep quiet about what he had seen and what he said he knew, if I would make it worth his while.'

Quietly, he added, 'I sent him about his business with a flea in his ear and went to find my daughter and learn the truth of the matter. She had gone away a few days before to stay with my sister in Scotland. My daughter, Ruth, and I only got back late last night . . . and I will let her tell the rest of the story herself . . . as she wished to do so.'

He turned and held out his hand to Ruth, who had been standing rigidly some way behind him.

'Come along, love. It's alright. I'll stay here with you,' and the look he gave her was such a mixture of love and sorrow that I could have wept.

In a low voice she told of how Duncan had suddenly jumped out in front of her as she was riding through the wood.

'I had no chance of avoiding him,' she said desperately, 'I . . . I know I was riding at a gallop and it was the wrong place for that but . . . but I had no idea he was anywhere about.' She gave a dry sob. 'He was waving a great bunch of grass or . . . or something and Satan reared up in a fury.'

She hid her face in her hands and swayed and the coroner motioned quickly for a chair to be fetched.

'Please sit down, Miss Thompson. Do you want a glass of water?'

There was a hint of compassion in his voice although I saw it disappear later, as she continued with her story.

'I managed to quieten him and when I dismounted and went to the boy I saw . . . I saw . . . Satan must have kicked him and he . . . he . . . ' her voice was a mere thread and she lifted a face full of anguish. 'I knew he must be dead.'

There was a wail of heartbreak from behind me, where Mary was sitting with her aunt and some friends but they hushed her, for it was plain to see that there was more to come.

The coroner waited for a moment or two and then said quietly,

'But you have more to tell us, don't you?'

She nodded, miserably.

'Yes, I'll tell you everything. I was terrified when I saw what had happened. I didn't know what to do. I jumped back on my horse and . . . and . . . I was going for help . . . truly I was. I was going as fast as I could. Emma would have to be there just then.'

Her voice altered imperceptibly just for a fraction of time. I know I was in a very sensitive state but I got the impression of a touch of spite. It was gone in a flash and I put it down to my imagination and felt annoyed with myself.

'We crashed into one another and she went flying . . . and then, there she was lying on the ground.'

She put her hands up to the sides of

her head and I could see that she was shaking. Her father stretched forward from his seat behind her and gripped her shoulder, murmuring something, quietly. She nodded at his words and braced herself.

'When I saw Emma lying unconscious I think I . . . I went a little mad. It all just . . . just overwhelmed me . . . all I wanted to do was . . . was run away from it all. I held on to Satan and . . . and . . . I know it was wrong of me . . . but all I could think of was getting out of this terrifying trouble. Everything had been an accident. I thought if . . . if . . . I put the little boy by Emma, everyone would think it was her horse that had kicked him. They would know it had to be an accident . . . she . . . she wouldn't get blamed.'

She turned desperately to her father and he put his arms around her as she sobbed bitterly. I think many of us there knew that her last words had not been entirely heartfelt . . . I, for one, was sure that she had seized an opportunity to cast doubt and blame on me, probably hoping that I would be driven away from Croxfield and away from Andrew. She had so very nearly succeeded too. But I wasn't about to tell anyone at all of my thoughts. Those sleeping dogs could lie for ever, as far as I was concerned. Ruth would have to live with the tragedy now. Not me.

If I was right and she had taken hold of the opportunity, I was equally certain that she had very quickly regretted it and bitterly. Poor girl. What an unhappy disaster she had created for herself.

She was strongly censured of course for the part she had played and for attempting to mislead police enquiries, but Jack Thompson's action in bringing her back and her own undoubted courage in owning up to her actions, mitigated the coroner's comments. The verdict was, of course, accidental death.

Albert was led away to account for his attempted blackmail and I wondered what poor little Mrs. Pegg's reaction had been. I felt sure she hadn't known of that. If he did get sent to prison, I thought, she would probably be better off without him.

As we walked out, Mary came up to me and laid a hesitant hand on my arm.

'Mrs. Dane, I . . . I'm . . . ' and she choked and sniffed into her hanky.

I put my one good arm around her and whispered to her not to worry and we both shed a few tears, thinking of the little boy we had each loved in our different ways.

I was very glad to get home and finally shut the door on all the trauma of the past few weeks.

The school holidays drew to a close, my arm was at last allowed out of its sling and Pat Somers and her family returned from Canada. She breezed into my house the very next day, full of smiles as usual.

After greeting each other and I had asked if she had enjoyed her trip and consequently been given a blow by blow account of the wonderful time they had had, she asked about my 'holiday'.

'I bet you've had a real quiet time, haven't you?' she said. 'Nothing ever happens in this sleepy little place.'

'Ah!' I replied, 'Sit yourself comfortably, Pat . . . I think this is going to take all morning!'

The annual village fete had come and gone, such excitements as the Gardening Show and Harvest Festival were but memories. The harvest had been gathered in, leaving the stubbled fields ridged in brown and gold and with fine pickings for the flamboyant pheasants and more sober and secretive little partridges and I . . . well, I had settled back into school life with ease although I knew I would always have some sad little memories. Peggy came down to stay with us for the half-term holiday and we talked at great length about those few weeks which had been such a traumatic part of my life. Then, by tacit agreement, they were laid to rest, as it were, and spoken of no more.

Andrew and I were growing ever closer and I had never been so happy.

The weeks fled past and excitement was building up in my classroom with all the Christmas festivities to look forward to. Douglas nearly choked on his morning cup of coffee when I told him of my plans for the Nativity Play that my class was staging . . . for I had cast George as the Angel Gabriel! Perhaps an imp of mischief had put that idea into my head in the first place . . . but it worked. He was becoming a different boy. The enforced absence of his bullying father had most to do with this, I suspected and these days he looked better fed and clothed.

The weather had been getting colder but on this particular Sunday the sun was shining and returning us to a more mellow autumnal day. There were still asters and Michaelmas daisies flowering in Gwen's borders and the Virginia creeper still blazed its coppery red up the ancient walls of Croxfield Hall.

Jenny and I had been invited to Sunday lunch and we walked up the driveway hand in hand. I held on to her firmly for she was dancing with impatience.

'Oh, Mummy, I can't wait to tell them.'

'You promised,' I reminded her. 'I only said you could be the one to tell Auntie Gwen and Uncle Arthur if you promised to wait for my signal.'

She nodded solemnly. 'When you waggle your fingers like this?' and she demonstrated.

'That's right, sweetheart.'

I just had to pick her up and hug her . . . and we looked into each other's eyes and laughed.

Andrew must have been looking out for us, for he came out to take my hand in his. There was no way he could catch Jenny for she was flying ahead into the cosy sitting room where Arthur was sitting in front of a crackling log fire.

As Andrew closed the outer door behind us, Gwen came out of the kitchen, busily wiping her hands.

'Ah, there you are,' she said, with satisfaction. 'I'm just about to dish up,' and turned to go back.

'In a minute, Ma,' and Andrew took hold of her arm and steered her into the sitting room. 'Just come with us. We . . . er . . . Jenny . . . ' and he grinned down at me, ' . . . has something to tell you and I can guarantee that if she doesn't tell you within the next two seconds, she will surely burst!'

My darling daughter had heard his last remark and was giggling but her eyes were fixed on me. Solemnly I raised my right hand and waggled my fingers.

She stood very straight, aware of the importance of the occasion.

'Auntie Gwen and Uncle Arthur, I've got something very 'portant to tell you. Mummy's going to marry Uncle Andrew and I'm . . . I'm going to be their bridesmaid.'

Then she forgot all about importance and rushed across the room to fling herself at Gwen.

'And I'm going to have a yellow dress like Mummy's best one . . . unless I have a red velvet one . . . and it's going to be at Christmas . . . and it will be the best Christmas ever . . . and, oh, Auntie Gwen, isn't it all just lovely!'

And it was . . . just lovely.

★   ★   ★

As I sat by the fire that wintry evening, remembering so much, I heard the front door open, letting a squall of wind and sleet invade our warmth and voices chase away my memories. What welcome and eagerly awaited voices.

'Hi Nan.' That was Jake, Jenny's first born, always wanting to be the first in. 'Nan, it's going to snow for Christmas. Grandad said so.'

'Then of course it must.' I answered him and held out my arms for three year old Beth. 'Welcome home, all of you.'

My darling Jenny, and her husband Rob, another vet. who had come to assist Andrew with his practice and fallen in love with her in no time at all,

393

followed them in and behind them, my own dearest Andrew.

'Found them on the doorstep,' he said as he bent to kiss me. 'Thought you might like them for Christmas.'

'Can't think of anything I'd like more.'

We heard the sound of Arthur's wheelchair then and he came in with Gwen behind him. Both of them slower now and white-haired, but the loving smiles and keen blue eyes were no different.

Perhaps my perceptions were heightened with all the memories I had been dredging up but I looked around at all my family and thanked the fates, that I had once nudged, that they were well and happy. Fanciful idea or not, at that moment the cosy sitting room seemed to be filled with love.

. . . And my cup was full.

We do hope that you have enjoyed reading this large print book.

Did you know that all of our titles are available for purchase?

We publish a wide range of high quality large print books including:
**Romances, Mysteries, Classics
General Fiction
Non Fiction and Westerns**

Special interest titles available in large print are:
**The Little Oxford Dictionary
Music Book, Song Book
Hymn Book, Service Book**

Also available from us courtesy of Oxford University Press:
**Young Readers' Dictionary
(large print edition)
Young Readers' Thesaurus
(large print edition)**

For further information or a free brochure, please contact us at:
**Ulverscroft Large Print Books Ltd.,
The Green, Bradgate Road, Anstey,
Leicester, LE7 7FU, England.
Tel:** (00 44) **0116 236 4325**
Fax: (00 44) **0116 234 0205**

TO LOVE AGAIN

Jasmina Svenne

After a disastrous romance in her youth, Juliet Radley has given up hope of marriage and become reconciled to a quiet life as Amy Gibson's governess. However, despite her expectations, she grows attached to Captain Richard Gibson, her employer's cousin — the only house guest to treat her with consideration. But a new arrival threatens her happiness: the rakish Hugh Faversham is the one man in the world who can expose her darkest secret . . .

DISTANT SUN

Sheila Holroyd

When, unexpectedly, a free cruise down the Nile is offered to Cathy she thinks it's the answer to her holiday problems. All she has to do is see if there is any way of improving the experience . . . Instead, she finds herself in danger from unknown enemies who will stop at nothing to get what they want. How can she tell friend from foe? Who can she trust? And romance with a charming stranger makes Cathy's life even more complicated . . .

TAKE A CHANCE ON LOVE

Cara Cooper

Fleeing family tragedy, a new start working at Margrave Manor seems perfect to Marie. Matthew Hughes, the charming gardener, takes a shine to her, but Mrs Johnson the house-keeper resents her very presence. What's more, Mrs Johnson warns Marie that Matthew has a murky past. When the police are called to an incident, everyone falls under suspicion. Will handsome, commanding Detective Sergeant Martin solve the mystery, and could he finally be the man to mend Marie's broken heart?

THE ECHOING BELLS

Lillie Holland

In Germany Marnie Burness accepts the post of governess at Schloss Beissel. Her charge is Count von Oldenburg's daughter, Charlotte. Despite finding much to disapprove of at the Schloss, against her own principles she falls in love with the Count. Then, when Maria, the Count's wife, is murdered Marnie suspects his involvement. She leaves the Schloss, but will she ever learn the truth about the death of the Countess — and will her suspicions of the Count be proved right?